Una's Journey

BAILIE LAWSON

Una's Journey

ONE

The morning of September 7th started off not very differently from any other morning for the past couple of weeks. How was I to know that my life was about to change so drastically?

I woke up at 9:30, an hour later than I'd intended to get up, and two hours later than I normally woke up when I had a job. I jumped out of bed while still foggy from sleep and started doing stretch exercises, to prove I was being constructive and optimistic about my life. After putting on some water for coffee and taking a shower I pulled on my old jeans and a tee-shirt and only then checked my email.

Nothing! It was early yet though. Maybe a job offer would appear in my email later in the day.

Or maybe they would contact me via the postal service. I hadn't checked my mailbox yesterday. I had been carrying bags of groceries and hadn't wanted to stop at the mailbox before trudging up the two long flights of stairs to my apartment. I went downstairs now to check the mail, eternally optimistic.

The envelope was addressed to Kathleen Una Donaghy. I'd long ago dropped the "Kathleen", so this couldn't be from someone offering me a job I realized with disappointment. I saw that it was from a business address in Albany, one I didn't recognize, as I plonked the envelope unopened on the kitchen table.

I delayed opening it until I'd had one cup of coffee and an English muffin with marmalade. As I started on my second cup, I found a clean knife and slit the envelope.

Feniweather and Crumpell, Esq. wanted me to contact their offices about the will of my late grandmother, Kathleen Mary McCarthy.

Well, how odd! Nana had died a couple of months ago, on July 10th, but why would they want to talk to me? Did she owe money? I thought Uncle John had taken care of all the funeral arrangements and bills.

Certainly, Nana didn't have too many worldly goods. Her house in Albany was probably the only asset, and we had always assumed that she would leave it to her only surviving child, Uncle John. My own mother, her only daughter, had died when I was quite young, and my father had mysteriously disappeared shortly after, so Nana had been my family, had taken care of me in that house until I moved out to go to college, and then later New York where I had lived for the past two years.

Well, there was no point in sitting here trying to figure out what they wanted. I'd better call this Feniweather Company. I picked up the phone and after listening to the polite greeting from the other end I asked to speak to Dan Hanrahan, the man whose signature appeared at the end of the letter.

I was informed in the same polite tone that he was not available and was transferred to his assistant who didn't give me much more information, but unintentionally answered the question of why he had written to me when she announced that the reading of the will was to be next Thursday, the 12th, and since I was named in the will I should attend.

I then called Uncle John in Albany, who was somewhat impatient as he usually was – he always seemed to have something more important to do; but he invited me to stay at his house, saying "Mary and the boys will be glad to see you".

I might as well, I thought. I hadn't seen my cousins since Nana's funeral and hanging around in New York isn't helping my state of mind and isn't helping me get a job. A watched pot never boils and all that.

I departed on the train to Albany early on Wednesday afternoon and was picked up at the train station by two of Uncle

John's three sons.

The older of the two, Jack was just 18 and very pleased to be driving his mother's car. He was big and friendly with mischievous blue eyes. He was accompanied by Matt, aged 16, a somewhat smaller duplicate of Jack, also with mischievous eyes. His were grayish. Peter who was 12 was at a game practice and we would pick him up on the way home.

They reminded me of puppies. They were affectionate and playful and treated me like an older sister. They had no sisters, and I was an only child, so they were the closest I had to siblings.

At 24 I felt endlessly more adult and sophisticated, and thought of them as children. Seeing Jack drive, and quite competently I had to admit, was an eye-opener. He was growing up fast!

This was my first time back in Albany since Nana died, and my second time staying at Uncle John's house. When I came for the funeral, they didn't want me to stay at Nana's house on my own. I wanted to. I had my own room there that Nana had always kept untouched after I moved out.

Now, at Uncle John's, I was greeted by his little wife Mary. She was tiny, but her tininess was accentuated when she stood next to her very large sons, who all looked like their father. Her small stature however didn't stop her from barking out orders to her large sons.

"Peter, change your clothes and wash your hands! Matt, take Una's bag upstairs for her and make sure to shut the window in her bedroom! Dinner is almost ready".

Matt dutifully carried my small overnight bag upstairs for me and explained that the window sash stuck sometimes in the guest bedroom and his mother had trouble opening and closing it.

"I wonder why we all have to go to the reading of the will" he said as he threw my bag on the single bed with the pretty pink bedspread. "I mean, Nana only had the house, and I'm pretty sure she left it to dad".

"I know" I agreed. "She didn't really have anything else. Maybe she had a little money saved up and left us a little".

"Yeah, that's probably it," Matt agreed.

By the time I got downstairs Uncle John was back from work and greeted me with a warm hug.

"Was the train on time?" he asked cheerfully.

"Yes, everything went smoothly" I answered. "And I was picked up at the station by the newest driver in the family."

Jack was looking pleased with himself.

"How is everything in New York?" Uncle John asked.

"It is good! Busy of course!" I lied.

There was no point in saying I had quit my job and didn't have another one yet. John was good-hearted but would feel obliged to lecture me and to ask for detailed explanations.

Partly to change the subject I asked, "Do you have any idea why all of us need to be at the reading of Nana's will?" as I nodded in the direction of my three cousins now all seated at the dining table, waiting expectantly to eat, while their mother placed large dishes of potatoes and carrots in the center of the table.

At a subtle signal from her Jack got up and went to the kitchen counter and returned with plates of roast beef which he placed in front of his father, herself, and his brothers.

Uncle John seemed to have his attention distracted by the approaching food and answered my question absent-mindedly

"The lawyers have to keep things confidential, so we won't know until we get there in the morning".

There was some good-humored joking about good old Nana getting the boys out of classes for the morning.

"We wouldn't want you to miss too much" said Uncle John cheerily. 'We know how much fun you have at school. You can probably make it there by 11 at the latest".

TWO

The reading was scheduled for nine am the next morning.
There wasn't much talk at breakfast among those who were
already up. John silently read the newspaper as he munched on
toast and drank his coffee. Mary busily removed dishes from the
table and brought others back.

I was glad to sit silently, drink my coffee while I woke up.
The boys seemed to be sleeping until the last possible moment,
finally bounding downstairs, and grabbing toast or juice
unceremoniously.

Jack and Matt drove together, and I went with Uncle John,
Mary, and Peter in John's car. The law office was in an old
redbrick building in downtown Albany.

In the dark-paneled silent waiting room, to my surprise,
sat Nana's sister Josie and Josie's daughter Maggie. Our
greetings were subdued to match the sobriety of the setting.

I was never sure if Josie recognized me but nevertheless, I
approached her to kiss her hello and to take a seat next to her.

We didn't have a chance to sit, however, as the inner office
door opened as if on cue just as the last person – Peter - entered
the waiting room and we were ushered into Dan Hanrahan's
spacious office.

He was a pleasant grey-haired man in his fifties, who
smiled and shook hands with each of us in turn, even little Peter,
and ushered us to seats around the spacious office. He then took
his place behind his desk and produced documents which I
assumed contained the official will.

Before starting to read he glanced around at the group and

cleared his throat. It reminded me of one of those old British mysteries where the will would reveal some family secret. I was to discover I was half-right!

Uncle John and Mary, their three sons, Jack, Matt, and Peter, all sat to one side together. Sitting together on the couch towards the center of the room were Nana's sister Josie and her daughter Maggie.

Josie was 87, and her sapphire blue eyes could be amazingly clear and alert and alternately vague and lost in their own world. She floated in and out of senility.

She seemed alert enough at this moment, but that could be deceptive I knew. She could look like that, yet when asked a question would stare vacantly and not seem to understand a word.

Josie's daughter Maggie was a stocky, dark-haired serious-faced woman of about 50. Maggie was unmarried but had a boyfriend for many years. We never saw him. Sometimes I wondered if he even existed.

I was aware I had taken a seat to the left of the desk separated in space from the others, aware of my alone status. Since Nana had died, I had become increasingly aware of my parentless state.

The reading began predictably enough. Nana had left the house to Uncle John, as expected; some small amounts of money to each of his three sons, a couple of hundred dollars to St. Agnes Catholic Church, which she had faithfully attended for many years; $500 and some jewelry to Josie.

And some property in Ireland to me!

I gasped in astonishment, as my three boy cousins all left their seats and tried to high-five me at once., forgetting it seemed that this was a solemn occasion.

I glanced over at Uncle John who was grinning broadly at my astonished face.

"Did you know about this?" I asked him in amazement, trying to absorb this revelation that Nana had owned property in Ireland all these years and hadn't told me.

He nodded "Yes, but only very recently. I thought it could wait. It didn't seem necessary to talk about it at her funeral" he said.

That had been the last time I saw him, two months ago, and in fact the last time we talked. But he could have let me know since then. Obviously, he wanted me to find out this way.

What a dark horse Nana had been!

It took a little more time before it sank in that I now owned this property. And it took a little longer still before I could grasp that there were five acres and there was a little house on it too, all in County Cork. It was the house Nana and Josie had grown up in.

I was excited. The thought of me – a 24-year-old New York City apartment dweller who was currently unemployed – owning a house and land of my own! It was amazing!

Nana also left a sealed envelope, addressed to me in her own small, neat handwriting. I decided to save this to read alone. I'd been very close to Nana, missed her, and wanted to savor those moments of closeness the letter might bring me.

Josie and Maggie were invited to come back to Uncle John's for "a cup of tea and a visit" after the reading of the will. The three boys reluctantly departed for school.

Back at the house while waiting for the tea and scones, excitedly I asked Josie about the house in Ireland. In my excitement at the lawyer's office, I had failed to get even the most basic information about it.

Uncle John volunteered that it was the house Josie and my Nana had grown up in and it was near the village of Lockamore, in County Cork. This I already knew. Nana had talked often about Lockamore and had wanted to take me there sometime. Sadly, that would never happen now.

Josie's reaction was puzzling though. She was startled at first, even agitated by my questions.

"That place!" she exclaimed, shuddering. "Katey always loved the old place, but I would never go back. I never want to see it again. It caused many bad things to happen.".

Then she lapsed into one of her vacant-eyed states and no more information could be gleaned though I tried.

Maggie shrugged. Apparently, she had nothing to contribute. Maggie seemed disinterested in the house, and it was obvious she had gone to the will reading only to take care of her mother. She and Josie didn't stay long.

After they left, I was able to talk to Uncle John, who apparently had taken the entire morning off work. He reminded me that about a year ago, Nana's brother in Ireland had died.

"Yes, I do remember hearing about that" I responded. "We had just found out that Nana was ill and were worried about her, and didn't want to tell her, so I didn't pay much attention to that news".

John said, "Ben had been living in the house in Lockamore, and he had left the house to your Nana as the next of kin. She, Josie, and the brother Ben had all grown up there, but Josie and Nana had emigrated to New York when Nana was 17 and Josie was 15, Ben staying behind to work on the land. He had married, but his wife had died ten or twelve years ago. We assumed there were no children, since your Nana had inherited the house"

"So, Uncle Ben had no children?" I asked, just to be sure.

"We assumed that, though I don't recall anyone actually saying there were no children", John answered. "There is a lawyer in Cork handling things and Nana had been in touch with him. She has owned the property for the past year".

"It has been only for a year" I said, more to myself.

"And even less than a year since she knew she now owned the house, so it wasn't a secret she was hiding from you all your life" Uncle John answered.

"That's a relief" I said. "But it makes sense."

"But how do you feel about it?" I asked. "I mean, do you feel it should be yours?"

"No. I am happy with her house here in Albany. And I knew for a while she was going to leave the house in Ireland to you. It is fair."

What was left unsaid was that I was the only child of his only sister, and my mother would have inherited the house in Ireland if she was still alive.

Nana often talked lovingly to me of the old home, and often promised to go back to visit, but she never had. I felt sad now that she had never paid that visit.

I remembered how Nana would tell me stories when I was a child. She would talk about her brother Benjy and his friend Mikey.

"Like two peas in a pod, they were" she would say laughing. "Always up to mischief".

She never mentioned Benjy's wife or if he had children, but then her memories were of them as children, and she had left long before he married.

****

That night in my room at Uncle John's I finally broke the seal of Nana's letter. I had been saving it up to read for when I was alone.

There were three pages covered with her thin small handwriting.

Una, love,

When you read this, I'll be gone to my reward. You'll have to go back and see the old place for me. I always knew you'd have the same warm heart and feeling for the place as myself. Josie would never go back. And John would not fit in at all. He has no interest. I could never get him to go back to visit. He is more American than you, it's strange to say.

Well, Una love, try not to let the old place go out of the family, for there's no more family over there now since Benjy died. And it was a struggle in the old days to hold onto the place, that we shouldn't let it go in times of ease.

Mind too that there's always a lot of pishogues abounding in Ireland and I wouldn't be paying too much attention to them at all. Or to any old gossip either.

I always wanted to take you back with me to show you the place I was reared but now you'll be going in my stead.

Don't be grieving for me darling, for when it's time for me to go I'll be ready.

Your Nana.

How like Nana it was, - cheerful, calm, affectionate, matter of fact! I could hear her voice saying those words.

I was amused by her warning to ignore old gossip and

pishogues – pishogues being superstitions, one of those old Irish words that crept into her conversation often enough.   Did she think I would hear old pieces of gossip about her I wondered in amusement? Worried about her reputation, was she?

I didn't feel sad; rather I felt warmed by the communication with Nana that the letter brought. It was like hearing her voice again.

But how like her not to leave any money to use to get to Ireland! And here I was, out of a job! Well, I guess the trip would just have to wait another little while.

But she was right! I was excited, intrigued, curious. I really wanted to go and see where Nana had been born, where she had spent the first seventeen years of her life. And even though I had not seen the place I wanted to keep it because that was what Nana wanted me to do.

I had no idea how I would manage that, but I would figure it out.

THREE

I went back to New York the next day, somewhat relieved to get away from the boisterous cousins, all resembling Uncle John a bit too much for my liking, though I was fond of all of them, including Uncle John – and the little fluttering worried mother.

It was evening when I got back to my apartment - Friday evening. It was hot again, a return to muggy summer weather. I made some iced tea, found a can of tuna fish, and made a sandwich, turned on some music, turned it off after a minute, and contemplated my life. I was back to the grim reality of my jobless life.

I'd quit my job at the advertising agency two days after I had come back from vacation, almost two weeks ago.

Tim and I had finally decided to take separate vacations after discussions about going somewhere together didn't lead anywhere. That should have been my first clue, but I didn't see it until later.

We worked for the same company, Todd, McPherson, and Johnson – on different floors it was true – but with enough contact during the day. I had scheduled my vacation for the first two weeks of August and thought he was planning to do the same. When he announced that August was not a good time for him to leave the office, that there was a project that needed to be finished, I didn't push it – didn't ask for any details, accepted the explanation.

I had already scheduled my vacation with Human Resources and my boss, my grandmother had just died, and I had no energy for dealing with change.

I also had no plans for my vacation, thinking Tim would take care of plans. He had been so understanding of my frequent trips to Albany to be with Nana while she was dying.

We had been seeing each other for six months. It started out very light-heartedly, a fun-filled unserious fling.

At 24, I was beginning to want more stability, but I didn't want to appear too serious or clingy, so I convinced myself that I really needed space too, that a two-week break would be a good thing for both of us, that we would appreciate each other more as a result.

I ended up going on a trip with my friend Liz, who wanted to go to Cape Cod. I was out of ideas and was willing to let her take the lead. After two weeks of college boys in Cape Cod I was no longer pretending to myself that I preferred this to being with Tim. I was bored, alienated, and was anxious to see him. I had no premonition that I was going to be dumped.

He was straightforward though. I must admit that. We had a drink after work on my first day back and he told me he had started seeing Susan. Susan was the little blonde assistant who worked in the office next to mine - A friend of sorts, or so I had thought. She was very stylish, not too imaginative, restrained. Now I understood why she'd been too busy to talk to me all day – and the pitying glances of Mandy, the middle-aged kind receptionist.

I was calm – unexpectedly so. What was there to do? Nice, upright young man finds himself falling in love with young pretty blond. They are victims. It is not his fault. They just fell in love. He does the honest upright thing and asks to be excused from current (worn-out?) relationship.

What can I do except gracefully withdraw? Otherwise, I play the role of ogre.

We parted amicably. In fact, he was the one to act guilty

and emotional while I was calm and reasonable. Until I got home, that is, when I howled, pounded pillows, and got flamingly angry with Tim, Susan, and all the people in the office who knew all day and didn't tell me – who knew all week and didn't try to stop it. With no-one to see me I could be as emotional and irrational as I wanted.

Still darkly furious the next morning, I called Mr. Jordan and muttered something about being sick. I did the same the next day. And the day after that I decided I could get another job and I called Mr. Jordan and said I wanted to give my notice for "personal reasons". If he knew all about the personal reasons, he didn't mention them, but he was kinder than I would expect normally to someone quitting without notice.

I decided I needed the rest of the week off to recover and went out and spent recklessly at Bloomingdales on beautiful, imported clothes I couldn't afford.

By Saturday night I'd wound down. I went to bed early and cried. And I woke up on Sunday morning with vengeance in my soul. I'd show them! By doing something! I'd get a better job than I'd had! No more waiting patiently among the rank and file. I'd go get a job at what I really wanted to do – illustrations for children's books.

I was continuing my art courses at night, studying graphic illustrations, and working to try to pay my rent during the day. But I had never given up on my goal, and maybe I was using this blowup with Tim as an excuse to go for what I really wanted.

By Monday my long tantrum was over. I started to look for a job, but only got a few polite thank yous in response. I was getting despondent. I started working furiously on my portfolio. I churned out black-and-white drawings, one after the other.

I didn't quite know how to adjust to this time on my hands,

time I usually spent at work or with Tim. I reminded myself I had been complaining about not having enough time before to work on my portfolio, to seriously try to find more interesting work.

I knew deep down it wasn't that I really loved Tim that much. No, it wasn't a question of love; it was more a feeling of being insulted. After six months I had gone away for just two weeks, to come back to be dismissed. I was angry that he could discard six months of our lives so lightly. My ego was bruised.

Drawing was restful, calming, and it freed my mind up to think about what I wanted.

I had taken the job as a graphic designer at the advertising agency because I needed the money, and because I thought I would actually be doing graphic design. The money was useful, but the work was not creative in the way I had hoped. I had rationalized that I was continuing to develop my skills there as well as at my evening course at Pratt two nights a week.

When Nana got sick, I spent a lot of weekends in Albany with her, leaving on Friday evening and coming back late Sunday. I saw Tim on the weeknights I was not at my art class, and sometimes even after the classes. I was constantly busy.

I was starting to realize that being active was my way of blocking out the panic that had set in when I knew Nana was going to die. I didn't want to think, didn't want to feel.

After she died, I felt numb. On vacation in Cape Cod with Liz, I allowed her to take the lead and tagged along with her to the beach, biking, noisy bars, double dates. Liz was unhappily single and somewhat aggressive in her quest to date. I told myself I was just being a good friend, tagging along and helping her date, but I was not interested in these boys since I already had a relationship at home with a sophisticated charming man.

There was partial truth to that, but underneath I was fighting off feeling pain and grief at the loss of Nana. I had lived with her and my granddad after my mother died when I was four years old. I had lost her and my childhood home.

And now there was the place in Ireland! The place Nana had lived until the age of 17. It was her gift to me. – It offered a chance to get to know her past, a part of her life I really didn't know much about, and a way to stay connected with her. She had left a part of herself to me!

But she had taken away my childhood home and given it to Uncle John when he already had a home of his own. The house in Ireland was a tremendous gift, but it was in another country, and it came with strings attached. In her letter to me Nana had said that the family had held on to the place through bad times and she hoped I would hold on to it too. That was a huge responsibility and an expensive job. I didn't know if I was capable of doing it. I didn't know if I wanted to do it.

.

.

FOUR

Over the next few days, I felt anxious and uncertain. But gradually I started seeing things differently.

It was sinking in that Nana had offered me a part in this family, a sense of continuity, of belonging, a chance to connect with the past, to stay connected with family, as if she knew how lost I would feel after she had gone. She was leaving me a part of herself, her younger self

. And it was true that it made me feel I belonged somewhere. It made me feel stable. I owned a house of my own! I wanted to learn more about the family who had lived there in the past. I knew so little, only odd bits of information I'd managed to drag out of indifferent Uncle John and vague Aunt Josie.

Maybe the lawyers knew more. I had been so stunned at the news that day in the lawyer's office that I didn't ask any questions. Now I remembered that Mr. Hanrahan had given me his business card and said to get in touch when I had questions. I remember him saying that – "*when*" I had questions, not "*if*"! He must have seen that I was too surprised to ask for more information then.

I could call now. I should make a list of what I needed to know. I had so many questions! If Ben had died a year ago, and Nana had obviously not been there, then had the house been left unlived in for a year? Was anyone taking care of it? Was it in bad repair? Had Ben lived there alone? I thought he had been older than Nana and she was 89 when she died, so taking care of a house and land would have been a lot of work for an elderly man on his own. He must have had some help.

So many questions! I called the lawyers office and left a

message for Mr. Hanrahan to call me.

I had no money, but I now felt a responsibility to make sure this property was being taken care of. I needed to go there. I had time since I wasn't working but I had no money. I just wasn't sure how I could manage it.

Dan Hanrahan greeted me in a friendly way when he returned my call. He had had a few lively conversations with Nana, especially in the last year. His own mother was from Ireland, and he'd been there a few times. He had never been in Lockamore, but believed it was a beautiful area in County Cork.

There was a rustling of papers as he tried to answer my questions. "Last year, after Mrs McCarthy inherited the house, I was in communication with her brother's lawyers in Cork."

" Ah, here it is" he said after a pause. "Matthew O'Sullivan, in Cork city – he was your Uncle Ben's attorney, also his executor of his will. I have his address and phone number. Kathleen agreed that he should hold on to keys, and she arranged for him to pay someone to keep the house in good repair until she could get there herself".

He broke off and said in a quieter tone "She really intended going back when she first heard of your uncle's sudden death. Then when she became ill, she thought at first that she would recover and was just postponing the trip. Sadly, she never made it."

He said the last words in a regretful tone. I warmed to him realizing he had been fond of my Nana, that she had worked her magic on him.

I made up my mind then. Impulsively I said, "I want to go for her. I remember stories about the place from when I was a child. Even then she would promise to take me some day. I really would like to go right away but I have no money to even get there so it will have to wait".

I stopped, feeling embarrassed. I hadn't meant to share information about my poverty-stricken state.

There was a momentary silence and I felt even more embarrassed. Then he said something surprising.

"I would need to check this out with O'Sullivan, but the money in Ben's will to pay for upkeep of the house was transferable to your grandmother and should be transferable to you. However, there may be a stipulation regarding residency – the person receiving the money would have to prove they used it for upkeep of the house, and that they were living in the house at least part of the time. O'Sullivan would have all the details. I will check with him if you like".

"That's amazing" I gasped, and truly I was astonished. "Yes, please do. I would be very grateful for any information".

He said it could take a couple of days, but he would be back in touch as soon as he had an update.

This was sounding better and better. The house was being taken care of. It wasn't an old ruin. For the first time I realized that I had been assuming I had inherited a run-down thatched cottage, uninhabitable, and needing large amounts of money to renovate it.

I still didn't know what it looked like. Maybe it was a thatched cottage and rundown, and badly in need of repairs, but at least someone was doing essential repairs, so I imagined the roof wasn't leaking and there were no burst pipes. Furthermore, there was money available to pay someone now, and more money available to do more extensive upkeep, if necessary, in the future.

"There *may* be money available" I corrected myself. I can't be sure of that yet, until we hear back from O'Sullivan.

There was still the residency requirement. That might be

the stumbling block. Was I expected to live there permanently? It was all so complicated and overwhelming. And I still had the problem of lack of money to travel.

"Credit cards were invented for this type of situation" I thought recklessly, very aware that I had a substantial balance on my visa card presently and I might not be able to charge the airline ticket.

Nevertheless, I spent the afternoon, checking on the cheapest flights to Ireland, and double-checking my passport to make sure it wasn't close to expiring. My passport was good to go, and airfare prices decreased dramatically in October, rising again in November and December. I could get a much cheaper flight in two to three weeks than right now in mid-September!

Maybe this was fate, and I was meant to go in October! But I would wait to hear back from Dan Hanrahan before making any travel arrangements.

I was excited now and proceeded to search online for any information I could find about Lockamore, County Cork, weather in Ireland in October, distance from Cork City to Lockamore and anything else I could think of, that related to the trip.

By evening I realized I had not thought about Tim or my job hunt in hours. That was a very good thing. It might be escapism, but it felt good.

FIVE

Things moved quickly in the next few days. Dan Hanrahan had good news. Not only was there money available for house repairs, but there was a small monthly allowance available.

According to the provisions of Ben's will, I had to show proof of residing at the house to receive the monthly allowance, payable from Matthew O'Sullivan's law office. Dan wasn't sure of what kind of proof was needed, but he was sure it would be uncomplicated, and would all be explained when I got to Cork and stopped by O'Sullivan's office. I wasn't quite so optimistic, but I was open to possibilities.

He did provide me with the phone number if I wanted to call in advance. I did want to do that. I wanted as much information as possible before I left New York. I would be on a limited budget. I needed to know how much money they could give me and what I needed to do.

I felt very relieved after that first phone call. O'Sullivan himself answered the phone and warmly greeted me.

Well, so you will be coming here soon, will you?" he said. "I will be delighted to meet Benjy's grand-niece from America".

"I am hoping to arrive in a few weeks, in October" I answered.   "I am trying to book a flight, but they seem to have nothing flying to Cork directly from New York".

"Oh, you'll have to fly into Shannon. It is close enough," he answered.

"Yes," I agreed, "I can do that and probably get a bus to Cork. I will have to look into that".

"If you were able to arrive on a Saturday morning, I might be able to get someone to meet you at the airport and drive you back to my office" he offered. "You could fill out some papers and pick up the house key. We will give you directions to the house from here."

"Oh, that is fantastic, really nice of you". I realized I was gushing, but as he spoke, I realized I hadn't thought all of this through. I hoped I didn't sound incompetent.

I asked about the amount of the monthly "allowance" tentatively, but I did need to know. The amount he quoted was in euros which meant nothing to me. He said it would be enough to live on "modestly". He also agreed to go over the various house expenses, such as property taxes, heating and electricity bill amounts when I got there. His office had been paying those bills for the last year from a special fund that Ben had set up and that Nana had continued. We could discuss "how to proceed" as regards that when I got there, Matthew O'Sullivan said.

The business side of things was becoming more real and after the phone call I realized I had to think about how the house would be taken care of when I wasn't there. Up to now I had just thought of getting there.

Of course, I had shared with my friends the news that now I owned a house in Ireland. They were impressed, thought it was all very romantic. Genie suggested that I go and spend a few months there.

"You don't have a job, and they will give you money to live on while you are there. It's perfect!" she said enthusiastically. "Sublet your apartment and just go!"

"It takes time to find someone to sublet" I said doubtfully.

"I might know someone" Genie said. "A really nice, responsible person. I could ask her, but I know she is looking for an apartment."

I agreed. I saw that many of the flights early in October were selling out or were now more expensive than originally listed. I still felt I needed more time to think about the trip but realized I might have to pay a lot more money if I procrastinated. I booked the flight to Shannon for mid-October, leaving on a Friday and arriving early on Saturday morning, using my credit card to pay. I felt relieved after the reservation was finalized. I was really going!

******

I was becoming curious about Uncle Ben and wished I knew more about him. I searched my memory trying to recall any stories Nana had told me about him over the years, but nothing new surfaced.

I wondered had he been eccentric. Or was he simply very passionate about keeping the house in the family? Nana certainly wanted that, but Ben had really planned for it, had tried to set up conditions to make it happen, probably realizing that Nana would not outlive him by too many years. I wonder who he thought would eventually live in the house.

I thought he and Nana had written to each other occasionally. I wondered now for the first time if she had ever mentioned me as someone to inherit the house when she wrote to him. Had they discussed it at all? It had been important to them, but then again, they never talked on the phone; never saw each other in 70 years. There were just the occasional letters.

Once I had asked her why she never went back and she said it had been so painful to leave the first time, and "in those days it was so expensive, and then I was married, with the children". She had trailed off and I hadn't asked why, after John and my mother were grown-up, why she hadn't gone then to see her brother.

I had learned at a young age that Nana just wouldn't talk about things she didn't want to share, and it was useless asking.

Again, I was mystified that Josie was never considered as a possible inheritor by Nana and apparently not by Ben either and she herself seemed to feel revulsion at the mention of Lockamore. Revulsion and even fear I thought, remembering her reaction when I had tried to talk to her about it after the reading of Nana's will.

Josie's daughter Maggie would have a greater claim on the house than I had, but she had been silent the day of the reading as she often was. I found it hard to know what she thought about anything, but she hadn't seemed at all interested in the house, or in Ireland for that matter. Her main concern on the day the will was read was to chaperone her mother. She went back to Uncle John's house with all of us, but it really seemed to be done more as a social necessity. But then I had no idea what went on in her head.

Uncle John himself had obviously been pleased, had enjoyed my surprise, and had known for a while. I could surmise that he and Nana had talked about it. I could imagine Nana saying to him:

"You're my son and you will have my house. But I can't forget Annie's daughter. I only had two children. You never had any interest in Ireland, but Annie did, and Una does, and Benjy wanted someone to have his house who would want to be there. So, the house in Ireland will be Una's"

The conversation would have gone something like that. Only I wasn't sure what was said after that, and why they didn't tell me then as soon as the will was drawn up. I needed another conversation with Uncle John.

SIX

I had planned on having the conversation on the phone, but I ended up seeing Uncle John a few days later. He had found some letters he thought I might like to see – letters from Ben to Nana that he had found stashed away in Nana's house. He offered to send them, but I decided to visit, since there were also some of my belongings still in my bedroom – I still called it my bedroom – that I should go through.   They were thinking they would sell their own house and move into Nana's house.

"No rush of course" Uncle John said gruffly. "But we'll need all the rooms for the boys".

I said I understood, and I did. I hadn't lived in Albany for 6 years and had my own apartment in New York – not to mention a whole house in Ireland!

Still, I was sad at the thought of clearing out my belongings from the little bedroom that had remained virtually the same since I was a child; that Nana always kept for me so that I would have someplace to go home to.

I still had my housekey so I told Uncle John I would go to Nana's house directly from the train station and start clearing out. He would pick me up on his way home from work and transport me back to his house for dinner.

I should have expected this, but it was so final. As I turned the key, I knew this would be the last time I would come here. I felt cut off, adrift.

The house still felt so like Nana. It even smelled like her – a little flowery, a little sweet, a faint whiff of lavender. I looked at the old flower-patterned armchair by the window where she liked to sit and pictured her there, glasses perched low on her nose, a piece of sewing in her hands, eyeing me curiously, ready to comment on whatever piece of news I brought home with me.

She had been the one constant in my life, my true family. I felt bereft and choked back tears as I made for the stairs.

I should get busy packing up my belongings. I didn't have that long, only a few hours before John arrived.

I wondered what they would do with Nana's armchair, with her furniture. I didn't want to ask, didn't want to know. I wanted to remember this house the way it was now, the same way it was throughout my whole childhood.

I wouldn't come back after my uncle and cousins moved in. I wouldn't have a room anyway.

For a moment I paused on the stairs thinking that they needed my childhood room for "the boys" but in their present house they had a spare room I could sleep in whenever I was in Albany. Why was there no room for me now at Nana's – at my real home?

Uncle John had seemed pleased that Nana left me the house in Ireland, but did he think that was enough for me? That I didn't need to be able to come home to Nana's house?

I felt abandoned all over again. It was silly because truthfully, I didn't want to spend much time visiting my uncle and cousins. It's just they were all the family I'd got.

I forced myself to focus on clearing out my room. It still had the white coverlet on the bed, and the small bookshelf against the wall, crowded with books.

There was nothing in the bureau drawers and just a couple of old sweatshirts hanging in the closet.

I packed up old books, some of them left over from

childhood. I should throw them out, but I didn't want to. There were even some toys and games from childhood at the back of the closet that I had never thrown out.

I filled some cartons that someone had dropped off downstairs with the childhood books and mementos I couldn't bear to part with. Once the room was clear I could store some boxes in the attic temporarily until I could arrange to take them. I wrote my name with a black marker on the top of the boxes. I wrote "Una's Books" on the cartons with the books. I hesitated when it came to labeling the toys and games and just wrote "Una" - "Una's Toys" sounded ridiculous.

I carried the lighter boxes up the narrow stairs to the attic. The heavy boxes I left by the attic door for one of my cousins to carry up. Other smaller things I packed in my backpack to take back with me to New York.

After one last look at my bedroom, now already unfamiliar in its emptiness, I gently closed the door and went downstairs to wait for Uncle John. I sat on Nana's chair and hugged myself. The small blue pillow she used as a headrest still smelled faintly of her and stirred up strong memories. My tears flowed unrestrained.

When I heard the car pull into the driveway, I hurriedly wiped away the tears and stuffed the blue pillow into my backpack. I was smiling and cheerful when John strode into the hallway.

"All set here?" he asked. He looked tired. I could tell he just wanted to be home, have dinner, put his feet up.

"Yes, I'm ready" I answered. "I left a couple of heavy boxes for the boys to take to the attic."

"Fair enough. Let's go then" he said.

I waved a silent good-bye to Nana, to my childhood bedroom as I thought of how Nana had always been there for me and was still taking care of me.

I knew Uncle John really meant to be there for me too, but it wasn't the same. The house wouldn't be the same. My old bedroom would be gone. I didn't want to see the house changed and occupied by my cousins. This was a final good-bye. But it would all be okay.

SEVEN

In the car I told Uncle John that I was going to Ireland in Mid-October. If I could work out the finances with the lawyer in Cork, I would stay there for three months, since I had someone who would sublet my apartment for those three months. Uncle John kindly offered to give me some money to help pay for the flight. I was embarrassed, but accepted it as a loan, promising I would pay him back when I had figured out what I would do to earn money. My credit card was close to maxing out, so the extra cash might be necessary.

At his house he gave me a large envelope with the letters he had found. There were five or six letters, all in their original envelopes, some of them with Nana's name and address written in ink that was quite faded with age. They were all from Ben. I quickly looked at them that night in my room.

When I took the first letter out of its envelope, I saw it had the date written on the top right-hand side. They were all dated in the same way, so I arranged them chronologically, planning to read the oldest one first. I was so curious to know more about Ben, this man whose house I now owned.

The oldest letter was dated "4th May 1950". I thought I had read incorrectly, but after a quick calculation realized that 1950 was plausible. Nana and Josie would have been in the US about a year, having arrived about 1949.

The envelope was addressed to *"Miss Kathleen O'Loughlin, 1239 West 50th Street, Apt. 20K, New York, NY"*.

I recalled that Nana and Josie had lived in New York when they first came from Ireland. In fact, she had met Grandad in New York and had only moved to Albany shortly after my mother was born.

I read on:

"Dear Kathleen,

It was grand to receive your letter with your good news. Thanks very much for the dollars. They were useful in buying more livestock. But no more dollars now please. Look after yourself and Josie. I am glad the journey over wasn't too bad and that your boss is nice, and you like your job. It's good news too that Josie is coming out of herself and feeling better. I was worried about her when ye were leaving. It was the best thing for her.

It was lonely after the two of ye left. The house was very quiet. Mam is always talking about you and sends her love. Dad is quiet as usual, still trying to work but not up to it lately. Myself and Eileen are still going strong, but we haven't set a date yet. She is good company for Mam. Finbar Clohessy is helping more with the farm.

Look after yerselves,

Your brother Ben"

He must have been 19 then I thought. I wasn't sure exactly, but I thought he was older than Nana by about two years.

They were poor I thought. Nana was trying to help out by sending them money, but I knew she had worked as a servant in a big house when she first arrived in New York. She wouldn't have had much money.

I wondered why Ben was concerned about Josie.

I continued to the second letter:

May 19, 1952

Dear Kathleen,

I hope Josie has recovered and that they were able to help her at the hospital. Her nerves were never great and worse after the incident here. I was hoping it would all be forgotten now after all this time.   I heard Frank and his young family are emigrating to Boston.

The rest of the letter contained details of more neighbors and other details, having to do with farming. I scanned it quickly to see if there was anything else about Josie. Why was she in the hospital? And what incident? When there was nothing, I moved on to the next letter.

"11ᵗʰ November 1960.

Dear Kathleen,

I am sorry to be so long in answering your last letter. I have bad news for you. I'm sorry to say that we buried Dad last week. It was an ease to him. He wasn't well at all for months. Mam is quiet but her health is fine. Myself and Eileen got married last year.

We were all delighted to hear that you got married and to receive the wedding photos. Mike looks like a fine strong fellow. I knew you'd find a Yank for yourself. Maybe you'll bring him home for a visit one of the days."

There seemed to be a page missing. I looked in the envelope again, but it wasn't there. I noted that the envelope was addressed to Mrs. K. McCarthy, 1953 West 54ᵗʰ Street, New York, NY. Of course, after being married, they had moved to another apartment.

I calculated the dates. My mother had not been born yet. I wondered if Josie still lived at the old address, then. I wasn't sure when she married. Her husband, Eamon, had died at a young age and I had never met him.

The fourth letter, again addressed to the West 53rd Street apartment was written in 1967:

9th October 1967

Dear Kathleen,

I am sorry to be so long responding to you. It was a busy harvest, but the weather stayed dry, thank God. I have Tomas Nagle helping me these days. He is Seán's young son, a fine strong fellow of 18 now.

Eileen has been laid up these past few weeks. She lost another baby and took it hard.

Your own little Annie is the picture of you at that age. Thanks for the photos of the two of ye. I am glad Josie is keeping well too.

Your loving brother Ben

I decided to read the rest of the letters on the train back to New York. I was anxious to read them, but wanted to concentrate, and I was getting sleepy. It had been an emotionally draining day.

*****

Next morning, after a flurry of good-byes and John's invitation to visit any time and "look after yourself over there", I looked around with mixed feelings as Jack started to drive me to the train station.

On the train I took the manila envelope containing the letters out of my bag. It was quiet and uncrowded on the train, so I could read without distractions at least for now.

5 May 1969

Dear Kathleen,

I hope you and family are keeping well. Everything is as well as could be expected here at the moment. Eileen is still very sad, as indeed am I. It is a hard thing to lose a child. He was very sickly for quite a time.

I hope Josie is all right. I still worry about the incident here and that she has put it behind her.

I stared at the page. The incident here? Something happened before they came to America that caused Josie some distress. I hurriedly turned to the next page but nothing more was said about Josie. Ben continued with good wishes to Mike, Annie and John and promised to write soon.

The train made its first stop and I saw through the window that a large group of people was getting ready to board. I put the letter back in its envelope and gathered up the unread letters from the vacant seat next to me and put them back in the large manila envelope. I would finish reading them when I got back to New York.

EIGHT

I struggled into the apartment with my two heavy bags, packed with salvaged items from my past life at Nana's house.

The answering machine was blinking. Before checking my messages, I put the letters in their large envelope carefully into my desk drawer. I would have to wait to read them later.

Genie's friend Sandra Bellucci had called. She wanted to sublet my apartment while I was in Ireland.   Genie had assured me that she was reliable and I hoped she would like the apartment. I invited her to come by to see the space and to meet me. She was free that evening, so we agreed on 7:30.

I had a few hours to clean up a bit. The apartment was not in bad shape. It was clean enough, but there were a few belongings scattered around.

More importantly, I had to make space for Sandra, figure out where to stash my clothes and other belongings which I was not taking to Ireland. I would be leaving in a little over two weeks and would be gone for three months – maybe longer I thought.

I tidied up as best I could, made myself a grilled cheese sandwich and some tea. That would do for dinner. I needed to shop for food, but I would wait until tomorrow to do that.

Sandra arrived promptly at 7:30. She was friendly and pretty, petite with wavy dark hair and large brown eyes. She was dressed in a pinstriped pink shirt and navy jacket and grey pants. Genie had told me she worked as a paralegal in midtown, so that my apartment in the East 60s would be very convenient for her. I had also told Genie that I just needed the rent and utilities covered. I assumed that she had let Sandra know how much I would be asking in payment.

She greeted me warmly when I opened the apartment door and looked curiously over my shoulder at the apartment inside. I led her in and showed her around immediately. If she didn't like what she saw, then there was no point in sitting down and working out details.

She did like it. The tiny kitchen and bathroom were neat and clean, thank goodness. I apologized for the overflowing stack of folders and papers on my desk in the small living-room; that and my clothes in the bedroom closet needed removing.

But it was a one-bedroom apartment with reasonable rent within walking distance of midtown. I had been lucky to find it. Anybody would, even with two steep flights of stairs to climb and a noisy street outside.

I said "I will empty out the clothes closet. I will be taking my winter clothes with me, and I will box up what remains".

Sandra interrupted "You could just put whatever you are not taking in cartons and stash them in the top shelf". The closet had two high shelves. The one on top couldn't be reached without standing on a chair or stepladder and so was almost empty.

Sandra pointed to the high shelf and laughed saying "I am 5'2". I am not going to put anything up there so that would be perfect".

Relieved, I said "Great. I will do that."

I asked if she would like some tea while we talked further. She agreed, and we returned to the kitchen where I showed her my selection of teas.

"Of course, help yourself to all of these".

I opened the closets over the sink, where I had a few cans

of soup, and packages of staples, of salt, jars of herbs.

"I don't have much really as you can see but use anything you want".

While we sat at the kitchen table drinking tea Sandra told me a little of her story. She was working for a large law firm in the East 50s as a paralegal, and she would be delighted to live in my apartment as she could walk to work from here. She was presently sharing a large apartment with two others in the west nineties by Riverside Park.

She had been unhappy there for the past few months due to a recent addition to the group of roommates, a boyfriend of one of the original roommates, Adele, who was the original renter of the apartment. She didn't go into details about why she disliked the boyfriend, but said she started feeling uncomfortable there and really liked the idea of having a place to herself.

I asked if she was okay with this not being an official sublet, and she was agreeable. I would pay the rent bill online from Ireland, and she would pay me two month's rent in advance and mail me the third month's rent in two months.

She was getting out her checkbook as we spoke.

I gave her a keyring with keys to the apartment and the main outside door and my extra mailbox key. She would open the telephone and utilities bills when they arrived and write her own checks in payment. I wrote down the address of O'Sullivan's law firm in Cork and my cell phone number as well as my email address.

"I shouldn't be getting any other mail" I said.

"Other than junk" she agreed. "If anything looks important, I can email you and then send it to you in Ireland".

"Great", I responded. "It is odd not to know the exact mailing address of the house I inherited – my house, but it is one of the many things I didn't do yet."

I was feeling pleased. This was all working out well. Sandra was someone I could easily be friends with.

She asked with interest about the house in Ireland and I told her what I knew. I even talked about my disastrous past few months – Nana dying, discovering Tim had been dating someone at work and how I had quit as a result, and then discovering I had inherited this house.

Before she left, we agreed that she might drop off some of her belongings a few days before moving in.

I said, "You have keys, so feel free to drop things off after work even if I am not home".

I called Genie a little later to say thank you and it was going to be a good arrangement for both of us.

Genie said "Sandra is a really nice person, too nice sometimes. Did she tell you about that scum-bag, Lou?"

I said "No. Who is Lou?"

"Her ex-boyfriend!" Genie answered. "They were trying to work things out, were still together when he started seeing Sandra's roommate. Next thing Adele announced Lou was moving in with them".

"That is dreadful" I responded. "I would have been out of there immediately. I couldn't even work in the same building as the guy who cheated on me".

Genie knew the full story of me and Tim.

"Sandra is extremely tolerant. She always tries to see the other person's side of things." Genie continued. "She probably tried for a while to get along with them".

Genie went on to say she had known Sandra from High School. They had both grown up in the same town in New Jersey – I think it was Newfield – and renewed their friendship when they both found themselves in New York.

After that I thought of continuing reading Ben's letters to Nana, but it had been a long day. It was only ten pm, but I could hardly stay awake, so I staggered off to bed and sank into a long deep dreamless sleep

NINE

It was a good thing that I threw myself into preparations for my trip the next day. I still had two weeks, but I started to organize my belongings – those that would be boxed and stored in the top shelf of the bedroom closet and those things I needed to take with me. I spent a couple of days doing that and it was a good thing as I received an unexpected job offer on the third day.

In late August after I had quit my job, I had sent my resume to several publishers of children's books stating I was free to work on projects. One of them had responded to me and wanted to see my portfolio!

The email, from Brooks and Cole Publishers, came from Silas Van Dorn, editor, Children's Books Division. They were interested in commissioning drawings for a book for preteens. Would I call to make an appointment?

After my initial panic that I couldn't take a job right now, I reread the email and realized that they were proposing freelance work. I would do the illustrations in my own time and send them to them. That's usually how it worked. In other words, I could probably do the drawings in Ireland and send them to them. If I got the job, that is!

This was the kind of opening I had been hoping for. This first chance could lead to more of this work. I was excited.

After calling and scheduling an appointment I got busy adding extra illustrations to my portfolio. The receptionist at Brooks and Cole was not able to give me further information about the book or the kinds of drawings they wanted, but since I had two days before the appointment, I should use the time to prepare.

I did some extra drawings of trendy pre-teens in urban environments, outdoorsy preteens hiking, camping, etc. I added some drawings of woods, country roads, and cityscapes. Finally, weary from trying to anticipate what was needed, I decided they would either like my style or they wouldn't. They would see that I was versatile enough to do what they required, or they wouldn't. I had done what I could.

I felt excited and optimistic the morning of the interview with Silas Van Dorn. If I started getting commissions for book illustrations, I could be on my way to a much more interesting career than the non-career track I had been on at the advertising agency.

On the way to Brooks and Cole, as I thought about my former job it dawned on me that I hadn't thought about Tim in ages, and in fact I no longer cared about proving anything to him. If I got this job, it was for me alone. That was a good feeling!

Maybe I would even start to feel grateful to Tim's cheating for being the impetus I needed to catapult myself out of that job. I wasn't quite at that point yet though.

When I met Silas Van Dorn, I was taken aback. I realized I had formed a mental image of an older thin sanguine man with dark hair and a black pointed beard. The real Silas was in his early thirties, blond, muscular, quite good-looking in a preppie kind of way. He also was more approachable, friendlier, than I had anticipated based on the somewhat formal and business-like email exchanges.

The receptionist had asked me to take a seat in the waiting area. She would let Silas know I was here.

He emerged shortly from a nearby hallway, walking briskly, smiling, extending his hand in greeting.

"Glad to meet you, Miss Donaghy – Una, is it?"

I nodded yes, muttered something in greeting and he added

"I am Silas. Let's go back to my office and we can talk".

The office was small and overcrowded, with a large desk piled high with papers and books, a bookshelf that was similarly overcrowded, and a round table which was empty.

He pulled out a chair at the round table for me saying "Have a seat here" as he sat in the chair adjacent. "I see you have your portfolio".

As I opened the portfolio and laid the drawings on the table he said "The book is in one of the final drafts. Normally illustrations are incorporated earlier, but the author recently changed her mind about the book's message and so we are looking at different artist's work. This is a story about a young boy who wants to be an artist, so the author thought it would be interesting to include some drawings that the character has done."

I glanced up with interest. I liked that story.

"It is an interesting concept" I said, but I would need to know what he is thinking, what he is attempting to accomplish".

"Yes" Silas agreed. "Whoever is hired would be given sections of the book, but I can't do that until the author has agreed, the artist has been hired and has signed a contract. This is to protect the rights of the author".

He was busily examining my portfolio as he talked. He looked at the latest additions with interest, the drawings of urban trendy youths.

"I like these a lot" he said. "May I take photos of these to show to the author"?

I agreed, thankful that I had put in the extra effort over the past few days.

He took photos of some more drawings, said he could send me digital copies, then took out some copy of earlier drafts of the book, selecting a paragraph describing the boy's image of his unfriendly classmates whose heads turned into cabbages.

I laughed with delight. "I would love to do these illustrations. I am already thinking of how I would do it".

Silas seemed pleased. "Let me see what the author thinks, but I think you might be the right person for this."

I had been so engrossed in the idea of the drawings that I had neglected to mention the important issue of being out of the country for an extended period. I hoped this would not be a problem.

I started tentatively. "I am really interested in this project. I am assuming I would be working at home and sending you drawings".

Silas nodded. "The illustrations can be photographed and sent as email attachments. For the finals we would need the originals or even good Xeroxed copies can be sent in".

"So, if I am out of the country in the next few months, it wouldn't be a problem?" I asked.

"I don't see that as a problem. Even if the typesetters need the original illustrations, you could mail them to us – I would suggest registered mail and keeping good copies of them. But that would only be for the final version. There may be some back and forth. If the drawing doesn't match the author's vision you may be asked to alter it".

He looked questioningly at me. "That can sometimes be frustrating for the artist, but it happens. But yes, those initial illustrations would all be photos that you can send as email attachments to me".

I nodded my agreement, thinking I had a good camera I was planning on taking with me to Ireland anyway as well as all my art paraphernalia. Everything he had suggested would be very doable.

When I first had the idea to go to Ireland for three months my plan was to work on my drawings while there. Working on a project that I would be paid for was more than I dreamt of.

"Very well!" Silas was standing. "I will talk to the author and if she agrees then you will need to come back to sign the contract. I can then give you some paragraphs from the book for the first illustrations."

It was only when I was out of the building and standing among the jostling crowds on East 45th Street that I realized that I had only 8 days left before my plane took off for Ireland. Would they have made the decision by then?

It was foolish of me not to have said I would have to sign the contract in the next week. Then again it could have sounded too demanding. I decided not to worry about it. If I had already left maybe they could send me the contract.

Silas also hadn't said how many drawings would be needed or how much I would be paid. It would be spelled out in the contract probably, and I didn't care. Certainly, I could use all the money I could get, but what I needed more was to start building up a resumé, and a reputation as an illustrator of children's books.

As I walked back to the apartment, I started imagining what the house in Ireland would be like on the inside. Up to now I had pictured an old-fashioned cottage, perched on a hillside surrounded by very green fields, dotted with cows grazing. Now I started to wonder if there would be a room I could convert to my art studio.

Imagine having a whole house to myself!

TEN

Sandra called the next day and asked if I would mind if she brought a large suitcase of her belongings to drop off after work.

"Of course, that is fine" I responded. "Actually, if you would like to have some dinner while you are here, I will make some pasta – nothing fancy".

She sounded surprised and pleased. "How nice of you! I would really like that. I will bring some dessert."

Her suitcase was indeed large and heavy and bulging. I helped her carry it into the apartment. She looked tired and pale. As we ate dinner, I began to realize she was also quite tense and seemed stressed, not just tired from lugging a large suitcase from the upper West Side.

She relaxed a bit as we ate, was appreciative of the ravioli with store-bought sauce I had heated up. It wasn't fancy, but the Italian bread I had bought at the local bakery was fresh and went well with the salad I had made. I told her about my interview with Brooks and Cole and how I really wanted to work on the project. I could do it while in Ireland and would hopefully get more work as a result.

"Did you tell your room-mates you were moving?" I asked eventually. "How did they take it?"

"I told Adele. She is the one who holds the lease on the apartment. She didn't seem to care, but she's probably glad that I am moving" Sandra answered sadly.

She looked at me with concern. "I don't mean to say that I am such a terrible room-mate, that's not the reason she is glad I am moving. The situation is very weird. Her boyfriend who moved in recently used to be my boyfriend. We hadn't quite broken up when he started seeing Adele. I was still trying to deal with the relationship with him when she announced he was moving in".

"That is shocking" I said. "Did she even ask you if you would be okay with that?"

"No. She just announced it – which is more than she did when she started dating him. I discovered that when I came home one night to find them wrapped around each other on the living-room couch."

Sandra paused. "After I got over my shock, I did have it out with him. He said he thought we were over, so what's the problem? Of course, I thought we were taking a break from each other but trying to work out our problems."

"What a jerk!" I exclaimed indignantly. "Well, good riddance. You don't want him in your life".

She looked at me sadly. "Of course, I realized then that this was not a guy I would want to take back even if he was interested, but it was so insulting. Maybe I should have walked out right then, but I had nowhere to go. I started to look around for another apartment, and I am trying to spend as little time there as possible in the meantime, see them as little as possible."

"It's awful!" I exclaimed. "Didn't you mention another roommate also?"

"Yes, there is Valerie. She thinks it is all very bad, and she is supportive and good company when she is there, but she is hardly ever there anymore. She spends a lot of time at her boyfriend's apartment".

"So" I continued her thought "It is just you and them in the apartment a lot of the time. That is dreadful".

Moved by empathy for Sandra, I found myself saying "You know that couch" nodding in the direction of the couch in the living-room "it pulls out to a bed. You could sleep there tonight if you like."

Sandra's eyes widened. "Really! I could?"

"Why not?" I answered. "You probably have clothes you can change into for work in the morning. In fact, I have already cleared a lot of stuff out of the bed-room closet so you could hang some of your clothes up if you want."

Sandra's eyes filled with tears, and she hugged me. "You are so nice. Thank you. That would be great."

As I lay in bed that night I thought about Sandra and her situation. By the time I woke up in the morning I was convinced. I heard her moving around quietly, taking a shower. I staggered out to the kitchen to brew some coffee and was taking my first grateful sips at the kitchen table when she emerged from the bathroom wrapped in a large towel.

I waved in the general direction of the coffee-pot.

She mumbled "Great. I'll get dressed first" and disappeared into the bedroom.

"We will get along just fine" I thought. Mumbling and sparse conversation first thing in the morning was a plus. That is exactly how I like to start my mornings if I am forced to be around people.

When she emerged from the bedroom, dressed neatly in what looked like her work uniform, a variation of what she had worn last night – this time a white shirt under navy blazer and grey slacks – she grabbed a mug and poured herself some coffee, sat at the table, saying

"I have maybe 15 minutes. The great thing is I can walk to work from here. It will only take 15 minutes at the most".

"I was thinking" I began. "I will only be here for a few days more. Would you like to stay here for the next few nights? If you don't mind sleeping on the couch until I leave on Friday? Basically, you could just move in early."

She was pleased. "Mind? I would be delighted! You are sure I wouldn't be in the way?"

I assured her that I would have time during the day to do whatever I needed in the apartment. In fact, I had most of it done anyway.

Sandra was already thinking of how quickly she could completely move out of her old apartment.

"I would have to make a trip or two back to the old apartment to pick up the rest of my things. Maybe I could even take some time from work tomorrow morning when everyone will be out at work and go up there and get everything else. I could work late tomorrow night instead."

"They are flexible like that, as long as the work gets done by the deadline" she explained.

"That sounds like a good plan" I agreed. "You might never have to set eyes on those people again".

She hugged me before leaving for work. I was pleased to have done a good deed and felt I had found a new friend.

ELEVEN

I got a call later that day from Silas Van Dorn to say that I was hired for the project! I was thrilled but tried to sound pleased in a more professional way, rather than in an over-the-top adolescent way.

If I wanted to stop by tomorrow about 11 am the papers would be ready for me to sign, and he would give me some excerpts from the book for the illustrations. They were asking for three illustrations over the next two months. There could be between 8 to 12 illustrations altogether.

"I can't wait to get started" I exclaimed with a burst of enthusiasm, forgetting to maintain a more professional restraint.

That seemed to please Silas, however. He laughed.

"Yes, I think this will be a good collaboration" he said. "See you tomorrow at 11".

I did a little dance of joy around the apartment after I hung up. I couldn't help thinking Nana was doing her bit to help me "interceding with God on your behalf" as she would put it.   It certainly felt that my life had taken a turn for the better in the past couple of weeks.

I sat down at my drawing desk – I would miss this – and started sketching boys with cabbage heads. This might not be one of the first three illustrations needed but the image was so great, surely, they would want it in the book.

I drew a teacher in a classroom with a look of amazement and two boys with cabbage heads while other boys held their hands to their heads and stared in consternation. I was trying for a third head in the act of transforming and finally went for one where half the head was a cabbage and the other was still a boy.

I hesitated about drawing the boy protagonist as I wasn't sure how he was described and didn't want to develop a strong image that would be very different from the author's vision of her main character. That could be troublesome as I proceeded.

I left the unfinished drawing in my sketch pad. This would be coming with me to Ireland.

Only four days to go now. Not even four full days. I would be getting an overnight flight, arriving in Ireland early the following morning.

I started packing, partly to take my remaining clothes out of the closet and make room for Sandra's belongings, partly so that I would remember to pack essentials.

I was going for a good-bye dinner and drinks that evening with Genie, her boy-friend Jimmy, and Liz. It would also be a celebration of my new status as a free-lance children's book illustrator. I hadn't told them about this but knew they would be happy for me as indeed they were.

They were impressed with my new job title as well as with my homeowner status. Liz said she always wanted to go to Ireland.

I laughed and said, "Well you will have a place to visit now".

I added more soberly "Well, I probably have to do quite a bit of work to fix up the place first. It really is an adventure in that way. I don't know what to expect."

There followed some discussion of the difficulties driving in another country, about me needing to rent a car which would be expensive.

I had been so excited about the job with Brooks and Cole that I hadn't thought about all the responsibility I would have when I arrived in Ireland.

I would have no friends there. As I looked at the excited faces of my friends around the table, I started to feel homesick even before going. I didn't know anyone there.

I brushed it aside as I promised to keep in touch with them, to take lots of pictures and post them on social media for them to see.

*****

Genie and Jimmy insisted on driving me to the airport. Even though I protested when they offered, when it came time to leave, I was grateful. I had more to carry than I had anticipated.

They dropped me off with cheerful goodbyes and "we want details about everything", and I was left alone to start my adventure.

We eventually boarded on time and calmly, after enduring lengthy and confusing lines to check in and go through security.

As soon as the plane took off, I was filled with excitement and enthusiasm for this new venture. I thought of Nana and how pleased she would be. Hopefully Uncle Ben would have felt the same way.

I remembered that I had not finished reading his letters to Nana sent all those years ago. They were carefully stashed in my suitcase. If I had brought them in my carryon luggage, I could be reading them now, I thought impatiently. But then again it would have been difficult to concentrate, and I didn't want those old letters to get lost or damaged.

An elderly woman sitting next to me had said something to me as I sat deep in thought.

"Are you Irish or American?" or something like that. She had a strong Irish accent.

"I am American" I answered. "But my grandmother was from Ireland – from Cork" I added.

I had been around enough elderly people from Ireland growing up and anticipated that she would be asking those questions next.

Friends of Nana's of course knew where she was from in Ireland, but when we met new people, we were used to these questions. In fact, this woman looked a little like some of Nana's old friends.

She volunteered "I am from Tipperary myself, from Nenagh".

I nodded in recognition. I knew where it was on the map.

"Living in the States 30 years now" She was continuing.

"Is it your first trip?".

"Yes" I answered. "I'm going to Cork" I added, anticipating her next question.

After eating she closed her eyes and seemed to be sleeping. I didn't object to the friendly conversation but was glad that it didn't have to continue throughout the six hours of the flight.

I must have dozed myself. At least I closed my eyes and when I woke up it was getting bright outside. Confused I looked at my watch. It said 2:12 am. But it would be 7:12 am in Ireland. I decided to update my watch. I craned to look out the window, but couldn't see any land, just the beginning of dawn. I was sleepy but excited.

The plane started to make its descent and I could only see

fields divided by small walls. There were no tall buildings, no cities visible from the air. Of course, Shannon was a very small airport compared to JFK. I had expected that.

The airport was chilly and quite empty. The officials checking passports were warm and welcoming.

I gazed out the windows of the airport in wonder. I was in Ireland! I could only see parts of the airport so far, runways, planes, but I couldn't wait to get outside.

I would be met by someone sent by the lawyer Matthew O'Sullivan. As I waited to pick up my luggage, I wondered how I would recognize the person. But mostly I was relieved that I was here at last.

TWELVE

The person who met me was an astonishingly handsome young guy who was waving a sign with the name "Una" in large black letters on what looked like the lid of a white cardboard box. I saw him immediately. He was hard to miss, tall and with a loud voice.

When I stopped and looked in his direction he said, "Hiya Una, pleased to meet you. I'm Fergal,"

He extended his free hand and shook mine heartily while he pushed the sign under his other arm. He was friendly and casual, as if we already knew each other.

He took my luggage and led me out of the airport with dizzying speed, talking quickly as he did so.

"It is early enough so we might miss the traffic here, but we'll probably run into it when we get closer to Cork" he said cheerfully, not seeming that concerned.

"How long will it take to get to Cork?" I asked, walking briskly to keep up with his long strides.

I was at the same time looking around at my first view of Ireland. There wasn't much to see except other cars in the parking lot as he loaded my luggage into a fairly new-looking grey sedan.

It was breezy and a lot cooler than it had been in New York. But the light! It was different. My foggy, sleepy brain couldn't find words to describe it. But I couldn't wait to paint in this early morning light.

"Oh, about an hour and a bit" he said casually. "Is this

your first time in Ireland?"

I answered "Yes" and was about to explain about Benjy and the house, but he seemed to know already.

"I remember old Benjy" he said. "He would come into the office to see my uncle sometimes on Saturdays. I used to help out with the phones and the reception desk on Saturdays when I was still in school".

He opened the passenger door for me and laughed when I moved to get in at the left side. "Everything is on the opposite side here".

Once we were moving, he said, "Are you going to get a car?"

"That is the plan" I answered. "I am to meet Sullivan in his office, get the keys to the house, fill in some paperwork and then somehow get myself to the house, maybe arrange for a car, a rental or something."

As I talked, I looked out in fascination at the road and noted we were driving on the wrong side, and that the road was narrow and very winding. Driving here would be more challenging than I had anticipated.

"Don't worry" he said as if reading my thoughts. "The road up to your house is a small country road with not much traffic. You can get some practice driving on that before venturing further."

It turned out that Matthew O'Sullivan was Fergal's uncle, and the office he used to work in on Saturdays was O'Sullivan's law office. Fergal was presently a law clerk in another lawyer's office in Cork, having just completed his studies in law at the University in Cork.

"Oh, you are a lawyer!" I exclaimed.

"Only barely" he laughed. "I'm essentially an intern right now. It works differently than it does in the States".

"Shouldn't you be at work now?" I asked.

"It's Saturday!" Fergal laughed. "Uncle Matt asked me to pick you up and I was glad to do it. So here I am!"

He seemed to know everyone in Cork and offered to talk to someone who owned a garage about buying a good used car.

"I mean, honestly it would be ridiculously expensive to I rent a car for a few months. You can't do that. A good used car is the way to go. And you could probably sell it back to them when you are leaving".

I agreed cautiously. I needed to see what my financial status would be after I talked to Matthew. I explained the terms of Benjy's will wondering if he already knew since he seemed to know everything.

"I don't know what proof is needed that I will be continuing in Benjy's house" I said.

"I suspect that provision was written into the will because Benjy didn't want someone acting as an absentee landlord. He thoroughly disapproved of those. I don't think you will have to prove to Matt that you are living there. Believe me he would know if you were renting it out."

"Do you know the area well" I asked curiously. "I believe it is about a 45-minute drive from Cork City. Have you been there?"

"I haven't been to your house of course" he answered, "but I've been through the village, and I know the general area well enough. I grew up myself in Krumgedden – it is about a 25-minute drive from Lockamore".

He continued "There is a supermarket in Lockamore and a

hardware store. There are probably other shops that I have forgotten about. You will not have to go far for the basic necessities. But after you are settled in you will probably want to explore further afield".

"Yes, it will be exciting" I said. "What I am most anxious to see is the house itself. It is so amazing to actually own this house".

I talked a little about my grandmother in answer to his questions, and he talked about the history of the area around the time she had left.

"There was a lot of emigration from the countryside in the 1940s and 1950s" he said. "There was no employment anywhere."

We stopped briefly for coffee and a scone at a small busy restaurant on the outskirts of Cork. I badly needed the coffee at this point, aware that I had been traveling all night and it was now about nine am – or four am in New York.

I was too wired to sleep even if I had the opportunity right now.   I had three mugs of strong black coffee, nevertheless. I needed to stay alert. Being more wired was better than being less wired. After seeing Matt O'Sullivan, I had to get a car somehow and drive myself to Lockamore.

Fergal was one step ahead of me. He was making a habit of that I thought.

"After you see Matt, I could take you to the garage of a friend and see if they have a car they can lease or sell you".

"It is a long shot. Isn't it?" I asked. "I mean what are the chances they would have a car I could afford to buy?"

"I can phone them while you are with my uncle" Fergal offered.

I agreed that would help.

When we got into the city center, I looked around fascinated. It was bustling and colorful, and I really felt I was not in America.

It was hard to describe why exactly. The buildings were mostly old, interspersed with some very modern-looking buildings. The streets were narrower and not as straight as I was used to. It was funny to see so many stores with Irish names.

And the air felt fresh. It was breezy. There was something about the light too. There was a brightness. I searched for the right word unsuccessfully. "Bright" would have to do right now. But I was glad I had my art supplies. I would enjoy painting here in this light.

Fergal managed to park in an impossibly small space on the street between two other cars and we got out.

"We can leave the luggage for now. I will take you in to meet Uncle Matt."

The office was on the first floor of an old building reached by way of narrow dark stairs. There was a young female receptionist who looked about 17. I was reminded of Fergal's story of his Saturday job in this office while he was still in school.

"Hiya Brenda", Fergal said cheerfully. "Is he in?" Without waiting for a response, he walked past her and knocked on the door of an inner office.

A voice from within called out "Come in", and Fergal beckoned to me still standing by the reception desk and we entered.

Matt O'Sullivan stood up from his large desk and walked around it, hand outstretched in greeting.

"Miss Una Donaghy! I am very pleased to meet you", he

said as he shook my hand firmly. "It is such a pleasure to have a young O'Loughlin return and lay claim to the family property".

Fergal said, "I will be outside" and left, closing the door behind him.

Matt politely asked about my flight and what was my first impression of Ireland. He was a white-haired man in his sixties with sharp eyes that gave me the impression that he noticed everything.

He produced a large folder with documents for me to sign. I repeated that I had arranged to be in Lockamore this time for three months approximately, but that I had just received a freelance assignment which I would work on from here. In the future I may be able to continue to work from Lockamore.

In truth I hadn't thought about the future, and I wasn't sure why I had even said this. I probably was trying to impress on Matt that I did intend to use Lockamore as my home.

We agreed that the deed to the house would be kept by Matt for now, but I might want to put it in a safe deposit box in the bank once my account was activated and I was "set up".

I was puzzled, and it obviously showed on my face.

Matt explained, "One of the papers you signed authorizes me as executor of Ben's will to turn over his bank account to you. He used the Irish Independent Bank, which has a branch in Lockamore. You can cash checks or make withdrawals there. I have already arranged for them to issue checks in your name."

He produced a few books of checks and showed me my own name and the address of the house printed on them. He handed them over to me.

"I have already deposited the monthly stipend for October in the account, and there is a balance there to cover repairs and day-to-day expenses. I will continue to have the monthly stipend deposited at the beginning of every month."

"But if I go back to the U.S., would you stop depositing then?" I asked.

"No. The deposits would only stop if you rented or sold the house. That was Benjy's wish. He knew that anyone coming from the States might be back and forth. He really wanted it to be owned by the family.

Some time I will tell you what I know about the history of the house and the area, and what they went through in the old days. They had their share of trouble in the past".

I was fascinated. "I want to know now", I said, "but it would be better to hear about it when I can take it all in."

"There will be plenty of time Una" he said. "After you get settled in you can come in and visit and we can talk. Do you have a mobile phone that will work here?"

"Yes, I made sure to get a plan that could be used here. I don't suppose there is a phone at the house?"

"Well, there used to be" he answered, "but it has been disconnected. It might take some time to have the service turned on again, so it is a good thing that you have a mobile phone. I will give you a ring early next week and see how you are getting along."

When we had finished, Fergal was waiting in the outer office, as promised.

"I was onto Declan at the AI Garage" he said standing up. "They have a Nissan in good shape they could sell you, but it wouldn't be ready until later today. They need to do oil changes and other maintenance. If you want to see it now and like it, Declan would drive it over to you by about 6 o'clock tonight.

He says you could pay a deposit and have a few days to try

out the car. If you like it, you can pay the balance off every week and if you don't like it you can return it, deposit refunded, and they will try to find something else for you."

"That sounds fair" Matt said, nodding in approval "but go with her to see it, and then of course drive her out to Lockamore.

Turning to me Matt said, "You have a provisional license to drive here, don't you?"

"Yes" I answered, "And I am so grateful to both of you for being so helpful. You are making all of this much more manageable than it might have been".

Matt put his arm around my shoulders as he walked me to the door. "Ah, we'll look after you. You won't be alone" he said.

Fergal and I walked to the garage, which was a couple of blocks away, Fergal explaining that it was easier than looking for another parking space.

Declan was about Fergal's age I guessed, but quieter, more serious. The car looked decent, the price Fergal said quietly was reasonable. It was in Euros, and I had no idea if it was overpriced or even underpriced. But the fact that I could pay weekly made it a good deal.

Declan repeated what Fergal had told me earlier about having a few days to make up my mind.

"That's only fair" he said. "You need to have a chance to drive it and make sure you are comfortable with it. But I will make sure it is safe, in good shape. You won't have to worry about any mechanical problems".

Fergal added "Declan is the best. You can trust him".

I used one of the new checks Matt had given me to make a deposit, carefully writing in Euros instead of dollars.

Declan made sure he had the address of the house in Lockamore, and directions to get there, assured me it wasn't too far out of his way. He had to go in that direction anyway. He would be accompanied by a friend in another car, and they would both continue to Dunbrack – wherever that was!

THIRTEEN

On the road out of Cork to Lockamore I tried to be attentive to my surroundings, aware that I would have to drive on this road alone in the near future, but exhaustion was setting in. I wanted badly to sleep. It was about noon and 24 hours since I had woken up in my bed in New York.

Fergal had grown quiet too and I was glad I didn't have to carry on a conversation. I must have dozed off because I was startled when he said, "We are almost there".

We were driving past a small shopping mall.

"That's the one I was telling you about" Fergal said, "the local supermarket".

Then we were in the village. I spotted a large blue and white sign for the Irish Independent Bank next door to a hardware store. There were people on the street.   There was a bookstore. It looked much livelier than I had anticipated.

I started to pay close attention as we quickly drove out of the village. There was a fork in the road. We drove down the smaller, narrower road, following the arrow that said Doone Road. This was the road!

The address was Loonas, Doone Road, Lockamore, Co. Cork. Soon I would see the house called Loonas.

"It won't be long now" Fergal said. "You must be exhausted".

I admitted that I was exhausted, but also wildly excited to be seeing the house at last.

There were houses dotted along the countryside at irregular intervals, but the view was mostly of fields and stone walls.

"I think we are here", Fergal said as we approached a low wall with a garden gate in the middle. I couldn't see the house from my position in the car, but I could see worn lettering on the gate that said "Lo nas". He kept driving past the gate to where the wall ended and made a sharp turn off the road onto a paved parking area. Now I could see the house! It was right in front of us.

I jumped out of the car, tiredness forgotten, and stood staring. It was a grey stone house, with a dark gray slate roof – so not a thatched cottage. In fact, it was larger than I had expected. It was two story, with what looked like an out-house or shed at the back. There was a small path at the side leading to a closed gate which led into the back of the house. There were two small patches on either side of the small path that led from the gate up to the front door. There were weeds growing amid bushes of some sort. There might have been a nice small garden here at one time.

Fergal was staring too. "It is a good solid house" he said approvingly. "It is in good shape."

He had started taking my luggage out of the car.

I turned back to him. "Would you like to come in to see it?" I asked. "I don't know what is in there, of course, and I can't even offer you any refreshments."

"I will just walk in with you, make sure everything is okay in there" he said. "Then I should leave".

I got the front door key out of my pocket and put it in the lock. The door creaked as it opened. It was painted an unappealing dark brown with some of the paint chipping and peeling off.

"I will repaint that a different color" I thought.

We were in a long narrow hallway with stairs to the right. On the left was a small sitting room with old-fashioned armchairs and a sofa, a fireplace and two bookshelves. It looked cozy, well-worn, old-fashioned, but not neglected. I wondered if someone had come in and cleaned up recently.

I realized I had been holding my breath and let it out in a sigh of relief. "Well, if there is nothing else, at least I can sleep on the couch tonight" I said.

"Oh, it is probably fine in the rest of the house too" Fergal said. "Not modern but enough for your needs."

"Do you think someone might have cleaned up in here?" I asked. "I know Matt had said people were paid to do repairs, but I had expected it to smell musty to see dust everywhere."

"I would say Matt arranged for someone to do some cleaning recently".

We were in the kitchen now, at the back of the hall. He walked over to the stove and turned on the gas burner which immediately yielded a blue flame. Then he flipped on the light switch.

"See, he made sure that gas and electricity were turned on. Let me check to see if the heat is working ok."

I followed him out to the hallway where he consulted a panel on the wall which was blinking. "Yes, that is on too. Good job Matt. He thought of everything."

I went back to the kitchen and turned on the faucet. The water sputtered a bit, but then poured out without a problem.

Fergal was opening the fridge.

"Whoa!" he exclaimed.

Startled I looked around.

"There is food in here" he said.

Indeed, the open door of the fridge revealed milk, bread, cheese, butter, some wrapped white packages.

I was astonished, and so moved by this kindness that I felt tears fill up my eyes.

"I never expected this" I mumbled. "How caring and kind".

I realized I had been expecting a derelict old house and to have to camp out for a few days.

When we had driven by the supermarket, I realized I hadn't eaten in hours and wouldn't have a car to come back and pick up food for six more hours. I was moved to tears by the thoughtfulness of some stranger, who had gone to this trouble to make me comfortable.

Fergal looked into my eyes and hugged me spontaneously. I then sobbed on his shoulder. I was so tired, so overwhelmed by this kindness, by all the new experiences, but I felt at the same time that I was home in my own house, and that I had been welcomed home.

I mumbled something incoherent, not sure if I was communicating but he seemed to understand.

I broke away embarrassed. "I was expecting a rundown house and no-one to help me. I am just overwhelmed and overtired. Matt must have arranged for this," I said. "You have been so kind too. You have given up your entire morning. I can't tell you how much this means."

He hugged me again. "I am glad to help, I really am. It is an interesting story. You are brave to come here all alone."

He started to walk towards the stairs. "Let's take a quick look upstairs before I go".

I realized he was checking out the house to make sure it was safe. I noticed he was checking the windows in each room. I had not stopped to think of safety issues. But now thought if the house had been empty for a while, people might have squatted, tried to break in.   I might ask Matt if I should install an alarm system.

There were three bedrooms and a bathroom upstairs. Two bedrooms were furnished with beds and old-fashioned wardrobes. They were small. The third was even smaller and seemed to function as a storeroom, containing several cartons and pieces of furniture pushed in unceremoniously.

The sheets and pillowcases looked fresh and clean. They had been put on recently. I sighed again in relief.

Fergal seemed satisfied.

"It is a safe area" he said. "You don't have to worry about being here on your own. But since no-one has been living here, I was being extra cautious, making sure everything is safe."

We were walking back downstairs. "I'll be off then" he said, "but get in touch if you need anything".

I got my phone and entered his number into my contacts, sent him a text so that he would have my number also.

"When I am organized, you might like to come back to visit sometime" I said vaguely.

"Yes, of course. I'd like to see what you do with the place", he said. "If you are in Cork some time, we could meet up too. I can introduce you to people. Oh, and let me know how things work out with the car".

I stood at the door as he got into his car, waved, and drove off, then closed the front door and looked around the hall at my very own house.

FOURTEEN

I set the alarm on my cell phone for 5:30. It was 1:15, so I would get about four hours sleep before Declan arrived with the car. I crawled into the bed in the bedroom closest to the top of the stairs. I must have slept immediately.

I woke feeling rested but also ravenous. I remembered there was bread and milk in the refrigerator. I threw on the clothes I had been wearing - my suitcase was still downstairs - and made my way down to the kitchen.

The white packages in the refrigerator contained sliced meat – ham and some other lunch meat. There was also cheese. Happily, I made a large ham and cheese sandwich and had a glass of milk, again mentally thanking Matt O'Sullivan and whoever had done the food shopping. I truly felt welcomed.

When I opened closet doors in search of a plate and glass, I discovered a jar of instant coffee and a packet of teabags. These wonderful, thoughtful people had really anticipated my needs. I must find out who this person was who had shopped for me and thank them.

I filled the old kettle on the stove-top with water and when it boiled made myself a mug of tea. I brought it into the sitting room where I discovered I could sit in an armchair which gave me a view of the front gate and parking area. It was 6:15, but I wasn't expecting Declan to be exactly on time. I just wanted to be up and dressed when he arrived.

I splashed water on my face, ran a comb through my hair. I really wanted a shower but would wait until Declan came and went to do that. The bathroom was old, but clean and there were clean towels.

It was after 6:30 when the car pulled into the driveway, followed by another small tow-truck. I opened the front door, mug of tea in one hand. It was dark outside.

Declan held up the car key as he walked towards me. "Do you want to try it out?" he asked.

A young red-haired fellow emerged from behind the wheel of the tow truck and waved at me.

Declan said, "Johnny, move that out on the road so she can get out".

"It can wait" I said. "I'll just sit into the driver's seat now and wait until tomorrow to drive. It is dark, and I am jet-lagged, and I don't know the road, so I will wait until the morning."

I then added "I am sure it will be just fine for me, and thanks for bringing it all the way here".

"Fair enough" Declan said, as I took the keys and walked towards the car.

I didn't really need to sit in the car as I had done so at the garage, but Declan seemed pleased that I did. I turned on the engine and since Johnny had moved the tow truck, I moved the car back a few feet and forward, more for Declan's sake than my own. I was feeling sleepy again and tired, probably due to eating. I really was in no state to drive anywhere.

Declan gave me a card with the name and phone number of the garage before he left, and I promised to call if there was any problem.

After the tow-truck pulled out of the driveway I wondered if I should have offered them a cup of tea. I wasn't sure what the expectation was in present-day Ireland. My Nana would, of course, have been scandalized that anyone would be allowed to leave without being offered a cup of tea. But I was well aware that things had changed here in the fifty or so years since she had left.

I had been thinking of Benjy living here as I walked around the house, and particularly of his last days. Now I thought of Nana and Josie growing up in this same house. Maybe I would find traces of their childhood here. I didn't have anything particular in mind – but maybe old toys in the attic? Was there an attic? I hadn't seen any indication that there was.

But first I had to be practical! Tomorrow I would drive to the village, go to the super-market, explore the area, generally start to get my bearings.

Upstairs I unpacked some of my clothes and laid them over a chair to get some of the wrinkles out. I would deal with the old wardrobes tomorrow. I didn't want to open them now. Even though everything in the house so far was clean and neat, I still expected to find ancient belongings stashed somewhere and wasn't ready to see them yet.

Vaguely I wondered what had happened to Benjy's clothes and personal belongings. Of course, it had been over a year since he died, and Nana was the owner of the house after that. She or more likely Matthew Sullivan, the executor of his will, and obviously much more, had arranged to remove them.

Ben had left the house to Nana in his will, but there must have been other beneficiaries also, local friends. But Matthew had made it clear that the present contents of the house all belonged to me.

I found my nightgown and got back in bed again. It was 8:35. I slept.

****

When I woke, I didn't know where I was for a moment. It was dark. It felt like the middle of the night. My eyes gradually adjusted to the dark and I noticed unfamiliar shadows. There was an old-fashioned dressing-table, and the large wooden wardrobe that I had noticed last night and hadn't opened. I groped for my phone and saw it was 5:08 am – early, but not 3 am. I could get up.

But I didn't get up immediately. I lay there in a half-sleep, feeling that relief I often felt after dealing with a challenge, when I had no more immediate demands.

I had made the journey, found the house, got the car, learned there was enough money to live on for a while, people seemed welcoming and helpful. I had accomplished a lot yesterday. I could afford to relax a little.

But I hadn't texted my friends or even Uncle John to say I had arrived safely! I had simply forgotten. But I should get in touch now.

Texts were easier than e-mails. I reached for my phone and sent texts with the same message first to Uncle John, then to Sandra, and Genie and Liz.

The message was brief. "*Hi, arrived ok. House is great. Got a car. Will be in touch later*".

Okay! I was ready for coffee. Then I remembered there was only instant coffee. I would need a coffeemaker. I wondered if the hardware store I saw in the village would have one.

In the kitchen as I filled the old kettle with water, I thought that this was definitely one that Benjy had used. I had found other pots and pans in a corner closet, all looked well worn. The mugs and plates were old, several with small chips. I selected a white mug without chips.

I sat in the kitchen drinking my coffee and looked around. It was functional but hadn't been updated in a long time. I liked the sturdy kitchen table and chairs. They were oak I thought and had been here a long time.

I didn't like the peeling wallpaper with its beige flowery pattern, or the beige and brown linoleum on the floor. White paint would make a big difference and a tiled floor.

Was I already contemplating painting and decorating? The answer was yes. However, it wasn't practical. I would only be here for three months, and I had the graphic design project to finish, and possibly more work to be sent to me from Van Dorn while I was here. And after that? I couldn't plan realistically further than three months. But I was already entertaining the thought of living here permanently. I knew it was too soon to think of permanence. I needed to live here for a while first.

I craved some stability, some permanence. And living in the house that my grandparents, great-grandparents, had lived in was comforting after the loss of Nana.   I needed to belong somewhere.

But instead of house renovations, I could start to make myself at home in smaller ways. What I would do first was find a place to set up as a workspace. I missed the desk/drawing board in my apartment, but I could surely find a surface that would work for me somewhere in this house. Even this kitchen table would do in a pinch.

I remembered that room upstairs, the room I thought was being used as a storeroom, with cartons and pieces of furniture. It seemed quite crowded and disorganized, but I had only glanced in briefly yesterday. I could explore it later. Maybe there was a desk or table in there and I could use it as a workspace.

Now I would have some toast, if I could find a toaster, and some cheese, and more instant coffee.

I remembered it was Sunday. Would that mean the stores would be closed? But it might also mean less traffic and a good day for me to get used to driving on the opposite side of the road, though Fergal didn't think I would have to deal with heavy traffic in Lockamore. Cork had looked challenging yesterday, however with its crowded narrow streets and unpredictable bends and signs.

Upstairs, I surveyed the two bedrooms, wondering which one had been Benjy's. I couldn't tell. They were equal in size, and both furnished similarly. The one I slept in last night had a window overlooking the front of the house and the road. It also had a view of mountains in the distance. It was a nice view. I decided I might as well keep it as my room.

I finally opened the wardrobe to find it empty but smelling a bit musty. I left the door open. The dressing table had a mirror on top and a couple of small drawers, also empty. I knew I should unpack properly but wasn't motivated right now. I compromised and took out toiletries and placed them on the surface of the dressing-table and put some larger things in the drawers.

There was one bathroom in the house, on this floor. It was clean and old in keeping with the rest of the house. I should try the shower shortly. I hoped there *was* a shower in the old bathtub. There was a shower curtain, anyway.

The shower looked like a newer attachment to the older bath, but it worked. The water sputtered at first as if it hadn't been used in a long time. There wasn't much shelf space either.

After my shower I stood at the entrance to the "storeroom". The cartons blocked further entrance to the room. They would have to be moved to get to the furniture. I couldn't tell from the doorway if the furniture was worth salvaging, or even what furniture it was. Maybe it had been left there in readiness to be thrown out.

There were a couple of chairs and a surface that might have

been a small desk, but I couldn't see the legs or the bottom part. That room would have to wait until later I decided.

I got dressed thinking I would walk around outside, walk to the back of the house which I hadn't seen yet, look at the boundaries of the property, see if any neighbor's houses were visible. In my excitement at seeing the house I had forgotten that it came with five acres. I wasn't sure how that was arranged and in what direction. Where were the boundaries of the property? Another question for Matthew Sullivan!

It was just getting light outside but was still too early for exploring the village. If I was hoping to do some shopping I should wait until at least nine am. Even then there may be no shops open.

There was a back door leading out of the kitchen. I hadn't opened it yet. Walking down the stairs I decided I would open the back door and go outside that way.

I walked back through the long narrow little hallway at the foot of the stairs towards the kitchen, past the door to the sitting room on the left. The kitchen door was straight ahead. For the first time I noticed a door on the right. It was at right angles to the kitchen door and in a small alcove created by the top rungs of the stairs overhead.

It was probably a broom closet or small pantry I thought as I opened it. I stared in amazement at the view from the open door. It was a study or library, perfectly organized for work. Perfect for me! There was a desk and a leather chair behind it. There were bookshelves lining the walls, an armchair by the fireplace, and a small round table in the corner. I eyed that table with delight. I could use that to do my artwork. I could set up my laptop on the desk.

Wi-fi! I needed that, probably that meant a landline also. I was excited. This room felt like mine already. This is where I would spend my time!

I started wondering about Uncle Ben. All these books!
This room! This man was a surprise. Those old letters to Nana
had made me believe the family had been poor, had lived in a
thatched cottage. I had imagined a very different person I had to
admit. And I hadn't finished reading all the letters. There was so
much to learn.

There was even a switch by the fireplace which turned on
an electric fire with realistic flames. That pleased me. I did love
real fires, but this was easy, and I didn't have to worry about
burning the house down.

I closed the door gently to what I now thought of as my
secret room and made for the back door.

Another surprise! The back door led to a small square
entrance space with the outer back door to the side and another
door straight ahead which contained a small modern toilet and
shower.

This looked like a more recent add-on. The shower looked
new and there were glass shelves. This is the shower I would use
in future.

The back "garden" wasn't a garden, though it might have
been at one time. It was overgrown. There were bushes, and a
tree, some plants - I couldn't tell what they were - that separated
what I assumed was the house property from a large field. I saw
cows in the distance. The fence didn't seem adequate to keep
them out of my property.

I wondered who owned the field and wondered when I
would meet my neighbors. They must all have known Benjy very
well. Then I realized that *I* probably owned the field. That was
why the fence wasn't so sturdy. I walked down to examine it and
saw that behind a bush that partly obscured it was a rusty old gate
leading into the field.

I wondered about the cows. There was no mention in the will or from Matt O'Sullivan that I owned livestock. They were so far away that they could be in another field. I should probably start writing down a list of questions to ask Matt. I didn't want to be caught trespassing on someone else's property. I decided that exploring that field would wait.

It was still early, but I might as well venture out in the car. I would see if the supermarket was open. If not, I could park the car in the village and I could walk around and get some idea of what was available there and when the various shops were open, including the bank.

FIFTEEN

Doone Road was empty of traffic. I had to remind myself to stay on the left, but it wasn't as odd as I had expected, because the driver's seat was on the right and that in an unexpected way served as a reminder.

At the fork in the road where Doone Road merged with the larger road, whose name I didn't know, a small white van came rumbling along from the opposite direction. The driver, a white-haired woman waved at me as she passed. I would have waved back but she had already passed me. I was pleased. People would be friendly and welcoming I hoped.

I was soon in the village which seemed quite deserted. I decided to keep going. I could park in the parking lot of the supermarket and then walk back and explore.

The supermarket was a little further outside Lockamore than I had thought. There were some residential side-streets along the way, lined with houses with small front gardens, and plenty of space to park. I could stop there on my way back and walk a bit if the walk from the supermarket seemed too lengthy.

I was a little anxious about parking right in the village as I saw no cars parked along the street there, but a few signs which I couldn't read. I assumed they were in Irish. I would have to learn a few words, especially words having to do with parking.

I was surprised and pleased to find that the supermarket was open. There were only a few other cars in the lot, and I found a parking spot easily. The drive had been effortless, only about six minutes, and I was relieved that it had gone smoothly. I felt a surge of confidence. I could do this! All of it!

The building contained more than the supermarket. In fact, it appeared to be a small mall, with the super-market taking up half of it and various small shops taking up the other half.

There was even a little café, from which wafted delicious smells of coffee and rolls. I couldn't resist. There was a selection of pastries all looking and smelling mouth-watering. I selected a raison scone with butter and strawberry jam and a large coffee from the smiling girl at the counter, found the right coins to pay her with only a small struggle, and took my second breakfast to a small table looking out on the square center of the shopping mall.

I could see many of the small shops from here. I might browse there before going to the super-market. There were people coming in and out though not too many. They were open, that was the main thing. I would look for a coffee maker and then go to the supermarket.

There was a shop called Hamptons that had dishes and kitchenware displayed in the window. That might carry coffee makers. There were several clothing stores also.

I finished my coffee and made my way over to Hamptons. It looked promising. There were colorful mugs and plates, pots, and pans. And yes! coffee makers! They were European – Italian. I studied the box for instructions. I couldn't see any others that looked more familiar. This would have to do.

On impulse I also picked up a large yellow mug. Time to start putting my own mark on that kitchen! A splash of color. The kitchen needed some brightening up. I used my credit card to pay as I still didn't have much cash in Euros. I would visit the bank in the morning.

Next stop, the supermarket. I was fascinated with the different brands of – everything. The aisles were wider and less crowded than in New York, and they sold wine as well as fresh bread. I was having fun!

I bought enough food to feed a family of four for a week, and a bottle of wine. I might have guests – maybe Fergal would come to visit! Again, I paid with my credit card.

Emboldened by my success, I drove back and parked right in the middle of the Village's main street. There were other cars parked there by now. I intended only taking a short walk to get my bearings and get a sense of the place.

The bank had hours on the door – they would be open at 9 in the morning. There was a pub next door to the bank called Johnny Dillon's, and next to that a small shop that sold newspapers, candy and milk, bread, and other food staples.

Across the street from the shop was the church. People were coming out. Sunday mass was just over I guessed. I stood looking at it as it struck me that Nana and Josie had probably been frequent visitors during their childhood. Benjy probably had attended the church throughout his entire life.

Nana had been a faithful supporter of St. Agnes' Parish church and school in Albany. I had accompanied her to church as a child, and of course had dutifully made my First Communion and Confirmation under her watchful eyes.

I was an occasional church goer these days - that is, I didn't object to going if required. I often was required when visiting family. When I moved away from living with Nana I had quite easily and without any pangs of guilt lost the habit of religion.

Now, however, I was drawn to the church. I crossed the street with the intention of looking inside. It was mainly because of Nana, because I was imagining her as a young girl entering the same doors.

Some older women on their way out nodded in a friendly way at me as I entered. It was dim inside the main door after the bright light outside and I almost collided with an older man who was standing just inside the door.

"Oh, I am so sorry! I didn't see you!" I gasped in apology.

I saw he was wearing a dark suit and a peaked cap and was leaning on a walking stick. A pair of bright blue eyes studied me curiously.

"Ah, I'm just taking my time" he said. "You're fine! Not at all!"

He spoke just like Nana. I realized this of course was the local accent. Nana had never lost hers.

He was speaking again. "You are a Yank, are you? Are you home on a visit?"

"Well, I just arrived", I answered. "My Nana was from Lockamore".

"Who was she?" he asked curiously.

"Kathleen O'Loughlin", I answered. "Benjy was her brother. He died last year".

The old man staggered back a step or two dramatically as he looked at me with amazement.

"You are Katey's granddaughter!" he exclaimed. "Sure, I knew her well, and Josie.   They never came back. And Benjy and myself were great chums."

He stuck his hand out.   "Seán Clohessy is my name. Pleased to meet you."

Then he continued thoughtfully. "But sure, you have no family left here now."

"No" I agreed.

"I am staying at Benjy's old house", I volunteered. "I am

going to be staying for a while."

"Is that so?"

He grabbed my arm with a strength I didn't expect and said "I'm just going into Johnny Dillon's for a pint. Come in with me. My daughter will be here in a half-hour to drive me home. You will have a chance to meet her too."

He wasn't waiting for an answer but had started shuffling out to the street still holding on to my arm. He seemed to have forgotten to use his walking stick but was carrying it in his other hand. I thought momentarily of the food in my car, but it was a cool day. It would be okay for a half-hour. Besides, I did want to meet people, didn't I?

We slowly made our way across the street to the pub.

"Don't you need to use your stick?" I asked tentatively. I noticed he was walking with a slight limp.

"I don't. It's Deirdre who insists. I sprained my ankle a while back but it's alright now", he answered. "Sure, I'm fit as a fiddle."

It was fairly crowded in the pub, but Seán made his way unerringly to a bench to the side with a small table in front and patted a chair for me to have a seat while he made himself comfortable on the bench.

There were various greetings exchanged with him, and one young guy said cheekily. "I see you found yourself a girlfriend Seán. Are you going to introduce us, or are you keeping her all to yourself?"

Seán ignored the comment, shooting a derisive look in the direction of the speaker, but when the bartender, a middle-aged man who was Johnny Dillon himself in the flesh approached us, I was introduced with great ceremony as Benjy's grandniece home from America.

Johnny had a booming voice. "Well Benjy's grandniece, you are welcome here. We were very fond of Benjy."

There were a few curious glances in my direction and people drifted over to talk to us.

There was a mixture of ages. Even a couple of the older women I saw coming out of the church earlier were here. One of them said curiously,

"Is it Katey or Josie was your grandmother? I used to know both of them. Of course, I was very young when they went away, but still, I remember them".

I explained it was Katey and that she had died a few months ago. There were expressions of condolence and comments about Katey and Benjy dying only a year apart.

Seán asked once about Josie. Was it my imagination or did he seem less warm about Josie's memory?

The time passed quickly. I was enjoying myself. I was glad to have been welcomed in here and thought I could easily come into Johnny Dillon's on my own in the future.

"Ah, here's my daughter" Seán said suddenly.

I looked up to see a white-haired woman approaching the table. I realized with surprise she was the woman who waved at me from the car as I drove down Doone Road this morning.

"Deirdre, we have a returned Yank here" Seán said. "This is Benjy's grandniece back from America".

I put out my hand to shake hands "Una Donaghy" I said by way of introduction. "I just arrived yesterday, and I am staying at Benjy's house".

Deirdre was friendly and interested. "Is it you that inherited the house then?" she asked. "I heard that one of Kathleen's family from America owned the house now".

I said yes and added "I am staying for three months and am planning to be back and forth."

"I hope you like it here" Deirdre said. "I know Benjy wanted to keep the house in the family."

"I love it already" I assured her. "But I have never been in Ireland before, so I have to get used to things."

"We live further out Doone Road, but not far from you", Deirdre said. "We have to leave now. I left the dinner cooking in the oven and just came down to drive Dad home. But I would love to have a chat some other time."

She was taking a pen out of her bag as she spoke and started writing on a paper napkin she grabbed from the table.

"Here is my phone number. If there is anything you need, give a ring".

I wrote my cell phone number down on another piece of the napkin, tore off the section and handed it to her.

"I just bought a coffee-maker" I laughed, so if you want to stop by some time for a cup of coffee, I'll be fully equipped."

I left with them amid cries of good-bye from some of the people who had stopped by the table to greet me earlier. Deirdre was parked directly outside the pub in a spot that looked illegal to me. I promised I would visit them as I continued to my own car further down the street.

"That went well!" I said to myself as I fastened my seat belt, feeling pleased with the morning's adventure.

SIXTEEN

I spent several hours organizing the kitchen and my clothes in the old wardrobe upstairs in the bedroom I had claimed as mine – settling in. It felt good. I was making myself at home in my house.

It started to rain later in the afternoon which I took as an invitation to retire to the "study" – the perfect room – where I switched on the fire and curled up on the couch. I had placed my sketch pad and pens on the round table at the side. I might start working on the project tomorrow. I needed to remember that I had a job and a deadline. But tomorrow was Monday. I needed to go to the bank, call Matthew too.

I gazed dreamily into the fire. The flames looked real, and it even crackled a little. To me it was perfect. Benjy must have spent a lot of time in this room.

And Nana! Had she spent time in this room? Or had it been furnished like this when she lived here? The room was part of the original house, unlike the downstairs bathroom which was a more recent addition. The bookshelves and fireplace all looked old, but I wondered if this had been another bedroom in the past. The upstairs bedrooms were not that big, even for a family of three children.

For the first time I wondered if there had been more children. Nana had always talked only about Ben and Josie, and I had always assumed there were only three of them. Now I wondered if that was the case. I had no reason to think that Nana would conceal that information, but then I had not been successful in finding out about my own father and his family. She could be very resistant when she wanted. Even if there were just three children, Nana's parents may have used this room as a bedroom especially in their later years.

I felt a wave of nostalgia for Nana, a sad sense of loss. How nice it would have been to have visited here with her, to even have met Benjy, and to have heard all about the house and the family first-hand from them.

For a second or two I felt completely alone – a twenty-four-year-old orphan with a house and not one relative in this entire country. Alone in the house in the quiet countryside! I had thought of myself as Irish for so long, having been raised by Nana. Now I felt very American. It was an unexpected feeling. Although this was my heritage, here in Lockamore, I had a whole other life too.

I missed my friends in New York already, and my apartment. Both had given me a feeling of belonging in those weeks after Nana's death.

I looked around the cozy room. Yes, I was glad to be here, I really was. But the house held memories, reminders of a family I had belonged to, a family who were gone, a family I knew very little about.

And I wondered again about my father and his family. They were from an Irish background too. - they must be, with a name like Donaghy. I could have family in Ireland – cousins. And I didn't even know where in Ireland my father's family had lived.

Maybe this fire and the sound of the rain falling outside, and the dark, were causing this weird melancholy mood. Or maybe I was just weary after my big journey and all that had happened in the past day or two.

****

I decided to set up my drawing materials. Sketching had

always been an outlet for me, not escapism exactly, but comforting and absorbing. I wasn't planning to work on my project for the book design, but I realized as I sketched that I was doing just that.

At first, I sketched aimlessly, but then saw that I had sketched the house and the road leading to it. Then I drew cabbages with faces, and young boys. I worked with total concentration and was surprised to find that several hours had passed and that I was hungry.

It was dark outside, but the rain seemed to have stopped. I stood up from the round table I had decided to use as my drawing table and stretched. It was time to go to the kitchen in search of some supper.

I opened a can of the soup I had bought this morning – chicken noodle soup, and cut a chunk of cheddar cheese, and some delicious looking brown bread from the bakery this morning.

Since the rain had stopped it was so quiet outside. I gazed around the kitchen. Yes, I needed to paint the walls here, to brighten it up. But not yet.

Now that I had started drawing, I was anxious to keep going. I would try to do that in the next few days.   I should be hearing from Silas soon and it was important to meet the deadline.

It could appear odd to a stranger, or even to a friend, that instead of exploring the countryside, the house, my property, I was contemplating losing myself in my sketching. But that had been my escape always. That was what I did when I needed time to absorb or time away from situations that were overwhelming.

I realized that I now felt overwhelmed. It had been challenging to get here, even to cope with being a homeowner. Now that I was here, I needed to withdraw into my sketching, to give myself some time to adjust to being here.

Tomorrow I did need to talk to Matthew and visit the bank, but other than that I thought I would not explore or venture out for a little while.

I still felt slightly melancholy as I made my way upstairs to bed.

It was strange and entirely unpredictable that I was so preoccupied with thoughts of my father and his family, now that I had arrived in the old home of my mother's side of the family, but I decided to not try to figure it out now.

SEVENTEEN

Matthew had made the interactions with the bank easy. I had brought some forms signed by him, which I then signed in the presence of the bank representative, a round-faced openly curious balding man with a friendly smile. He introduced himself as Tom O'Shea.

I already had some checks for that account given to me by Matthew. Tom O'Shea now informed me that I would receive a debit card in the next week to ten days and reaffirmed that the sum of 1000 euros would be deposited into the account on the first of every month.

I saw that the current balance was about 15,000 euros. I still wasn't good at figuring how much that was in dollars, but it seemed like a lot. Of course, that balance was for upkeep of the house, repairs, etc., and I didn't know yet if any costly repairs were needed.

That reminded me that I needed to ask Matthew if bills - utility bills and other bills - would be sent directly to me at the house now that I was in residence. I guessed that would happen as I now was being provided with funds to pay those bills. I needed to know if there were big bills, like heating bills and property taxes that would need to be paid on a regular basis and how much I should expect to pay.

Now that the signing of forms was done, and I was officially a bank client Tom O'Shea became chattier.

"I knew your uncle of course" he said. "He used to come in from time to time".

"I never met him" I admitted. "I am sorry I didn't, but my grandmother used to talk about him and talk about this place".

"The Loughlins have lived in this area for a long time" Tom said. "I am a new-comer myself, only here for fifteen years, but I have heard the stories of the Loughlins from the old days".

I must have looked puzzled because he added "You know, going back to the civil war and even before – the house was a meeting place".

I nodded, not sure if I should ask more questions. While I was trying to formulate a response, Tom's demeanor changed, and his tone became brisk and business-like. He rose to shake hands with me and assure me that I could contact him at any time if I needed any help with my banking needs. It seemed that I was being dismissed, and quite abruptly too.

As I turned to leave, I saw that a well-dressed couple were standing a few feet away looking in our direction but without curiosity. The man who looked to be in his forties, had dark greying hair and was wearing a grey suit and carrying a briefcase. The woman who looked younger, was dressed in a stylish black coat, wearing very high heels and a short chic hairstyle.

Tom approached them and I heard him saying "Good morning Mr. and Mrs. Venable. Will you come this way?" They were important clients I assumed.

I had been abruptly dismissed, but I didn't feel offended as I made my way out of the bank. I was very pleased to know that I would be receiving a regular income every month, and that there was a lump sum in the bank. I was feeling like a grownup property owner!

Tom's last words to me intrigued me about the house being a meeting place. I wanted to know more about the history of the house and the history of my family.

But first I needed to deal with the present. I hadn't even explored all my property yet – those five acres. I wasn't sure how far they extended. I didn't know what five acres looked like.

Matthew surely must have more information. Maybe he had decided not to give it all to me on Saturday. I couldn't blame him. I couldn't have taken it in then anyway, in my exhausted state.

I still wanted to absorb my new life slowly but felt better able to cope this morning. The melancholy of last night had lifted.

I would call Matthew as soon as I got back to the house.

****

It turned out that I just needed to make some phone calls to have telephone and WIFI services turned on as they had already been installed. It would take a day or two, but then I could use my laptop and have internet service. I didn't need a landline, but "it came with the package".

Matthew confirmed that I would now be receiving all bills addressed to the house, but I might have to change the name for some from Ben's name to mine. He would send me copies of the payments made in the past year for taxes and heating, etc.

He believed that Benjy had made some arrangement with a neighbor to rent out some fields, but there should be some empty acreage also. I was reassured that the cows didn't belong to me, but probably to the neighbor who was renting the fields.

I heard some paper rustling as Matthew asked me to "hold on a minute".

"Ah yes", he said "If you look at the last few statements from the bank – I will send you copies – there is a deposit every month from L. O'Riordan. I believe that is the neighbor who is leasing those fields. That was a long-standing arrangement, and I was not involved at all."

Matthew paused. "I would say it is wise to let it continue.

You do not need those fields and it is a source of income. Besides it is a good thing to have good will with neighbors."

I assured him that I certainly did not have any plans to change anything but would like to know which of the surrounding fields were truly mine to do as I pleased with. Matthew reminded me that he had given me a copy of the house deed and a little map of the property. He had kept the original in his safe at the office until I was settled, when I could put it in a safe deposit box at the bank.

I had, in fact, not looked at those papers, which were in a large envelope, pushed into the bag that still contained all the documents that I had needed for my flight to Ireland. I hadn't taken them out yet.

EIGHTEEN

I had the papers spread out on the kitchen table and was starting to look at the small map when the doorbell rang. I noticed it was a modern-sounding doorbell. I hadn't heard it before as no-one had called yet.

Curiously I made my way to the front door, wondering who my first visitor would be. A grey-haired man in a cap and very blue eyes was standing at the door. He regarded me curiously and then stuck his hand out.

"Miss O'Loughlin, my name is Liam O'Riordan. I heard you just arrived". He had a strong Cork accent. "Pleased to meet you".

"Pleased to meet you too" I responded as I shook his hand. "And the name is Una Donaghy. My grandmother was Katey O'Loughlin. Benjy was her brother".

"Ah yes, of course" Liam said thoughtfully. "Benjy used to talk about Katey and Josie, the other sister. My father was a great friend of Benjy's, and he knew the sisters too."

"Come in". I stood aside and gestured.

"Ah no, I won't" Liam said as he shifted from foot to foot and looked in the direction of his boots which I now saw were caked with mud.

"I'm on my way to the back field now, but I wanted to introduce myself. I'm the one who has been renting the fields from Benjy and hoping to continue from you too."

"Of course, you are the L. O'Riordan that was listed in the papers!" I exclaimed.

"That I am!" Liam responded.

"Well, I'll be glad to have things continue as they were" I said, "if that's all right with you".

"It is!" Liam nodded his head vigorously.

There was a brief silence and I wondered if Liam had been a little anxious that I might want to make changes and if that was why he had come by so soon after my arrival.

"Do you live near here?" I asked, to break the silence.

"Just around the next turn and down about a half mile, on Tubridy's Lane" Liam said. "The fields are not far from my house".

I had an idea. "Did you say you are going there now?"

Liam said, "I am, to look after the cows, and then I'm going home".

"Would you mind if I went down there with you, just to see where they are, and to see which land is free for me to use? I have a map, but it would be great to get a look and see the layout with someone who knows his way around here".

"That's grand, yes". Liam said in agreement "if you don't mind going in the van", as he nodded in the direction of the van parked in the driveway.

"I don't mind at all" I said. "I'll just grab my coat".

I was back at the door in a minute, having also changed my sneakers for a pair of boots, and noticed the mud-spattered van for the first time. It looked well-used.

I hopped up on the passenger side as Liam asked, "Are you going to move in altogether?" nodding at the house.

"I'm keeping it, not selling it. I'm sure of that. But I only found out about it a month ago and was able to arrange to come here for three months. I would have to go back to the States then and try to get things organized so that I could come back".

As I spoke, I wondered why I was trying to give people the impression that I would move to Ireland and live here full-time, when I wasn't sure yet if that was what I wanted to do. I had indicated something similar to Matthew O'Sullivan.

Maybe I wanted to convince them I was sincere about carrying out Benjy's wishes about no absentee landlords and not letting the house go out of the family. Maybe I just wanted them to like me and accept me as part of the community.

"Indeed, that would make Benjy happy" Liam said thoughtfully.

"There is so much I don't know about the house and about the history of the family" I said. "I wish I had been able to come here with Nana before she died. She would talk about visiting sometimes, but somehow it never happened".

I turned impulsively to Liam "If you remember any old stories from the old days, I'd love to hear them some time".

"Well my father used to tell a lot of old stories, but the fella you should talk to is Seán Clohessy."

"I met him yesterday, and I met his daughter".

"Well, there you are" Liam said.   "No better man than Seán for that".

He braked suddenly on an empty stretch of road. While we talked, I had noticed that when we had turned onto Tubridy's Lane we had encountered no traffic. It was a narrower road and there were no houses to be seen. We were now close to a large gate to a field where cows were grazing.

"So here we are" Liam said. "This field, and the one

beyond are the two I am using."

He waved back in the general direction of my house. "If you walk over that way, you'll see there is a strong fence to keep in the cows. There's a small gateway in the fence and a few feet further on is another fence, which is not so secure, but that fence surrounds your property that is not rented. You could even go back to the house that way. There are gaps in the fence so you can get through. It might not be a bad idea to get that fence replaced."

I was fascinated. "That's great. I just wanted to see where the boundaries were. And how big it looked."

"You could grow some crops there if you had a mind" Liam suggested.

"Yes" I said vaguely and wondered would I turn into a farmer and decided it was highly unlikely, but then again life was unpredictable.

"Well, I should start my rounding up now" Liam said, nodding in the direction of the cows.

"Thanks Liam" I called as I set out across the field in the direction of the gate in the fence that he had pointed out.

I stopped and turned back. "Oh, I can give you my phone number if you ever need to contact me".

"Ah yes, and I'll give you mine", Liam said.

As we each entered phone numbers on our phones I wondered if there was any place so remote that people didn't have cell phones these days.

The field was quite large, and I could see a second one that looked equally large on the other side just beyond. I turned to my right and walked in the opposite direction pointed out by Liam and eventually I saw a narrow turnstile, not a gate, and a narrow laneway no more than four feet wide outside. There was an old wooden fence on the other side, broken in places. This must be the boundary of my very own unleased land!

I stood for a minute in the lane looking in the direction of my house in the distance. Excited, I then walked down the narrow lane and saw that it took me onto Tubridy lane. I realized the land from here up to Doone road was all mine. The same old wooden fence extended as far as I could see along the edge of Tubridy Lane. Yes, maybe it was advisable to have a sturdier fence installed.

I decided not to walk up Tubridy Lane just yet, but to retrace my steps along the little lane and continue from the turnstile and walk back on the little lane in the other direction. I wanted to see how far back my property extended. Already I realized there was far more land at my disposal than I had anticipated.

The fence going in the other direction from the turnstile where I had come out of Liam's field didn't extend quite so far. The lane continued but seemed to get even narrower, but the old fence turned at right angles. I tried to walk along outside the fence, but I had to walk off the lane and into tall grass and eventually it was too overgrown.

And it looked a little gloomy too.

I retraced my steps back along the lane and soon found a hole in the fence large enough to squeeze through onto my property. I then walked as close to the fence as I could back to the corner of the property. There were some nice tall trees on my side of the fence. The other side looked derelict.

But there was a strange shape, like that of a tombstone, silhouetted against the darkening sky. It was at a distance, and I couldn't quite make it out. There were other shapes too that looked similar.

Was I living next door to a cemetery? They could be hedges or small bushes of course - or they could be tombstones. It gave me a queasy feeling.

I could see the house in the distance which was comforting as it was getting dark quickly and now it was starting to rain. It was just a light drizzle, but the combination of the late October gloom, the unfamiliar landscape and the lack of light was not appealing. I decided to move more directly towards the house and leave the exploring of the boundaries for another time.

I walked as quickly as I could across the uneven and overgrown ground and arrived at the back door of the house with still enough light to spare, but barely enough light to see by.

I was a little spooked at the thought of a cemetery so close and at the rapid arrival of darkness. I made a mental note to buy flashlights when I went on my next shopping trip. There were no lights where I had been walking.

Another half hour and I would have been lost in almost complete darkness. I hadn't even left any lights on in the house that could have served as a landmark to guide me back.

I fumbled with the keys on my keyring, guessing that the one I hadn't used yet was for the back door. It was. I let myself in gratefully, glad to be "home".

NINETEEN

That night I decided to explore Benjy's bookshelves. I pulled the curtains shut in what I had started calling "the study", turned on the fire and made sure the outside doors were locked securely. I started thinking again of getting an alarm system. Yes, I was a little spooked still from what I thought I saw at the other side of my fence.

I knew I was being illogical. If there was a cemetery next door, was I afraid of ghosts? And would secure locks protect me?

I would explore again in bright daylight, but I wondered if there were old books, especially local histories, that might tell me something in the meantime. I wanted a history of the house and of the village.

I had barely looked at the contents of the bookshelves before now. I had noticed before that there were volumes of literature – Yeats, Oliver Goldsmith, and some books in Irish. They were the most prominent, at eye level close to the armchair I had appropriated.

But when I hunkered down, I saw there were some dusty old books, and even some large folders on the lowest shelves close to the ground. I couldn't read the titles of the books, so I pulled them out, about seven or eight books and a large black folder and carried them over to the table. I pushed my sketch pad aside. I had left it there open, ready to continue drawing when the mood struck.

Now I sat and examined the book titles in the brighter light from the lamp that hung directly over the table. My instinct had been correct. These did seem to contain history and geography and they appeared to be very old.

I quickly opened the first pages of each in turn to get more details about what the book contained. There was one on the history of Cork City which I put aside for now. There were three that covered details of the townships in the immediate area, one that contained old photos of people and buildings, and one titled "Poets and Writers of West Cork".

I reached for the black folder. It was a plastic loose-leaf binder and there were typewritten pages inside as well as a pocket in the inside back cover that contained several envelopes.

This piqued my interest. It seemed personal. Was it a personal record of some kind?

I suddenly remembered I had not finished reading the letters written by Benjy to Nana all those years ago. How could I have neglected those?

The truth was I hadn't forgotten but I had been so driven to take care of pressing details and then I had been so overwhelmed that I had escaped into my sketching. But I would read them later tonight.

But now I would concentrate on this black folder and these books.

I took the envelopes out of the pocket at the back. There were several large manila envelopes, fastened with a clasp but not sealed. The envelopes looked old. Indeed, the black folder itself looked like it had been undisturbed in that bookshelf for a long time.

One envelope said "Mam and Dad" in faint blue ink on the front. The second said "Eileen." And the third said "Katey and Josie" in the same faded blue handwriting.

I opened the third envelope curiously. It contained photographs – very old photographs in black and white.

The top one was a photo of a very young Nana. She looked about five or six years old, but that smile, and those eyes were the ones I had known so well. She was wearing a white dress and a veil. I realized it must have been a photo taken on her first Communion – she must have been about 7 then, maybe 6 at the youngest. I was happy to see I was right when I turned the photo over and saw some writing on the back.

"Katey's First Communion, May 1939".

I stared for a while at the young face with the infectious smile.

The next photo was a similar one of Josie. In fact, the dress and veil looked the same. They probably were! They would have been saved for the next girl's First Communion.

Josie looked happier and more – alert – was the word I was searching for, than the Josie I was familiar with.   Her smile was more tentative, not as infectious as Nana's.

There was also one of Benjy. This was the first time I saw a photo of him. He had blond hair and a solemn face, no smile. I realized with a shock that he resembled my Uncle John quite strongly, except John had dark hair. Flipping to the back I saw that this was a photo of his Confirmation in 1942. Of course, in those days they would not have taken so many photos. Mostly they would have been taken on special occasions.

But there were others, and more casual photos too. The next one was of four girls of about ten years old in summer dresses sitting on a long bench. Two had braids, and the other two had long dark hair held back with a wide band. I thought those two were Nana and Josie, though the photo was blurry, and I couldn't be sure.

The next one I had no trouble recognizing – at least my Nana and Josie. Nana was a poised teenager, wearing a pretty dress and was beautiful.

I stared at the face, so familiar and yet different realizing she had never shown me photos of when she was young. Why had I never seen photos of her when I was a child? She must have had some. She had no photos, not even of my mother or of me when I was very young. And it was odd I was only realizing this now.

Josie was smiling in the photo and her eyes were very blue. She was looking up adoringly, I thought, at a tall good-looking older boy. He was wearing an open-necked shirt and a vest and was leaning on a fence looking straight at the camera. He was probably in his late teens.

The photographer had captured an instant, a visual memory, that told more than just words could. Josie had had a crush on this boy. I was sure of it. And they were still in Ireland. I couldn't be as sure of that, but I thought so. Nana and Josie looked so young, and the road that stretched behind them was narrow and winding.

Who was this boy? Curious, I flipped to the back. All the other photos had names and dates on the back, so this one hopefully did too. Yes, there was something written in the same faded blue handwriting. But I stared in astonishment at what it said.

"Katey, Josie and Frank Donaghy, June 1949".

But Frank Donaghy was my father! Why was he in this photo with Nana and Josie in 1949? I was confused and it took me a second to realize that this couldn't be my father. I remembered from the times I had tried to get information about my father that he had been born in 1966.

So, who was this man? Could he be a relative, an ancestor of my father? Could he be my relative? And if the photo was taken here in Lockamore or somewhere close by the chances were that this Frank Donaghy lived locally too.

Nana had never mentioned that Donaghys lived in Lockamore or nearby. She appeared to know nothing about my father's family when I asked her as a child and as a teenager. If she knew a relative of his while in Lockamore, surely she would have told me. It must be just a coincidence. It had to be. What else could it be? Donaghy was probably a common name in Ireland.

Still, it stirred up my curiosity. The man in the photo was probably dead now. He looked older than Nana and Josie in this picture. But it was likely he had lived locally. If there were still Donaghys living in this area, his relatives, I could find out about them, maybe even meet them.

As I grew older, I had decided that Nana thought it was idle curiosity on my part to want to know so much about my father, that it wasn't important, and besides my questions seemed to bother her. For those reasons I had convinced myself that in fact I didn't need to know. Maybe as a child I wanted to keep a close relationship with Nana. After all she was all I had. I didn't want her unhappy with me.

As a child, I understood without being told that discussions of my father were off-limits. I learned to keep my curiosity to myself. But now I wondered again why Nana was so reluctant to talk about him.

Now though that I was alone – I didn't really feel that Uncle John and his family were my family in the same way Nana had been - I felt I had the right to as much information as I could find.

I was beginning to feel that there had been an oddness to the lack of communication from Nana about the past – not only about my parents, but even about this house in Lockamore. I puzzled over it now.

I took the photo containing Frank Donaghy out of the pile and placed it on the table.

There were more photos of a young married Nana with my grandfather and baby John. I felt sad for Uncle Ben, here in this house never seeing his sisters again and just having these photos. Of course, he had a wife for many years, and in the early years his parents were alive still. I knew it was more difficult and more expensive to travel in the past, but couldn't they have visited occasionally? I tried to imagine an existence without emails, even phones, where letters could take over a week to arrive. I shook my head. No, that was one aspect of the past I would not like.

The final photo was of a beautiful girl of about 7 or 8 with large eyes and long dark hair. I knew before turning to read the writing on the back.

It was my mother! Those eyes! That hair! They stirred long-dormant memories in me, and I remembered her face. I actually remembered her real face not a photo of her face! Because this was the first photo, I had ever seen of her. That was an astonishing revelation to me.

I wondered yet again why Nana had no photographs, and why I hadn't been more curious about that when growing up. Why hadn't I asked to see photos of my mother? Surely, she had some. Maybe I had asked when I was very young and just forgot that I had asked.

I took that photo out of the pile and placed it on the table next to the one of Frank Donaghy. I knew he wasn't my father, but it gave me something to hold onto, those two photos.

The other envelopes contained photos of Ben and his wife and of my great grandparents. Nana looked a bit like her mother and Ben looked like his father. Josie, I realized didn't look much like either of her siblings, though she might look a bit like her mother.

I was suddenly tired, exhausted, in fact too tired to even

sketch, so I went to bed and fell into a deep dreamless sleep.

Climbing the stairs, I realized I once again had not read the rest of Ben's letters to Nana.

TWENTY

I woke up early with images of a dark-haired little girl in a blue dress smiling at me. It was my mother's face from the old photograph.

I got up quickly and found the envelope with the old letters Benjy had sent to Nana, still in my suitcase, stashed in a corner of the bedroom, and took them down to the kitchen. I skimmed through them while I was waiting for my coffee to brew. But there really was nothing.

No, of course, there was something! He had written about life here in Lockamore. But I was looking for something to help me understand my mother or father. I reread the letters from the beginning, and yes, I had seen it before – the letter dated May 19, 1952. He had written

I hope Josie has recovered and that they were able to help her at the hospital. Her nerves were never great and worse after the incident here. I was hoping it would all be forgotten now after all this time.   I heard Frank and his young family are emigrating to Boston.

Frank but no last name. When I read it first, I had been so focused on Josie and the mention of the "incident", and I hadn't paid any attention to the name Frank, thinking Ben was mentioning an old neighbor of theirs. That might be all it was, but when he mentioned other people, he always gave their last names too.

It was frustrating that he didn't mention Frank's last name. Did that mean they all knew him so well that there was no need to mention a last name?

I turned to the next page.

They have two small children now. I think they are going to Boston first but might not stay there.

Ben then continued with more updates on their mother's health and there was no further mention of Frank.

Did it matter if the man's last name had been Donaghy? He was Nana's age, even older. Why would he be related to my father? It was just a coincidence.

Being here had reignited my interest in learning more about my parents and it had been startling to see a photo of a man named Frank Donaghy when I had never even seen a photo of my own father of the same name. That is what made the most sense.

I sipped my coffee thoughtfully. Ben hadn't mentioned my mother by name, or John either, just said he hoped the family was doing well. And he hardly mentioned Josie in the later letters. He wrote more about her in the earlier letters. The last mention of Josie was when he said he was glad to hear that she was getting married and hoped "she would settle down and be happy now".

Again, I had a sense of things left unsaid about Josie, something that was understood by everyone but not put into words. Had they thought Josie had not been settled or happy up to now? Was I reading too much into a simple phrase?

But Josie had an aversion to Lockamore, hadn't wanted to talk about it the last time I saw her. I wasn't imagining that. Did something happen all those years ago? Something that made her want to leave and never go back?

I had always thought that Josie was just a little eccentric – when I thought of it, that is. Lately I had explained it as senility, but hadn't she always been this way, even when I was a child?

Now I was suddenly becoming aware of how many things were left unsaid in my family, how odd things happened and were not explained. It was the only family I knew so I had simply accepted it as a child. Now, maybe because I was on my own, at a distance from them, I was starting to question what I had taken for granted in the past.

It wasn't just Nana, but Uncle John and his wife, who didn't talk about the past or about my parents, who had no photos of them.

Maybe this questioning was spurred on by Nana's death too. I had literally been turned out of my childhood home. My childhood bedroom was being made over for one of my cousins. When Uncle John said matter-of-factly that they needed the space I had accepted it. I had even said that I had my own apartment and now I even had a house in Ireland, and I meant it. Or I thought I did.

Yet now I thought of how I was their only cousin. There was just me. Why couldn't they have kept a place for me, made me feel that I belonged to their family?

I didn't really want to be with them I suppose but was that partly because I had always felt excluded? And that had been my childhood home, the only one I remembered.

****

I was only four when my mother died. I did understand then that she had left me, that she had gone away, and I remember asking when she was coming back. I remembered a gentle sweet-smelling woman with long dark hair. I remember her lying in bed unable to talk to me. I remember asking her if she was sleeping and her not answering.

My father disappeared around that time. I had vague memories of him, tossing me in the air, laughing, then holding onto me very tightly and crying, so that it frightened me. Then he was gone too.

When I was about seven, I had started asking a lot of questions about my father, Frank Donaghy. I was told that he and my mother had met when they were very young.

"He took it bad when she died" my grandmother would say, always the same words. "He withdrew into himself and then took off".

After a while I stopped asking. He was not a part of my life.

When I got older, I realized I must have another grandmother, my father's mother, and other cousins besides Uncle John's sons - a whole bunch of relatives on my father's side. Nana was reluctant to tell me anything, so I stopped asking. Maybe the subject of my mother made her sad. That was how I understood it in my teens. Besides, when Nana didn't want to talk about something she wouldn't, and all the questioning in the world wouldn't make a difference.

That didn't stop my curiosity though, and as I got older, I became more and more curious about my father and his family – my family. I started to do my own research, starting in high school, and especially when I went to college. I was away from home for the first time then, in Burlington, and after heart-to-hearts with new-found friends, who mostly complained about their parents, and then felt embarrassed when they found out I didn't have any, I decided I would make use of the internet to piece together a story that Nana and Uncle John seemed reluctant to share with me.

I knew that my father, Frank Donaghy, was the same age as my mother, so that would mean he was born in 1966. If they knew each other from childhood he must also have lived in Albany, probably also went to St. Agnes Catholic School.

There was no Frank Donaghy to be found in the High School yearbooks for 1981 to 1984. I even extended the search back to 1980 and up to 1985.

He did not have a phone number or address listed anywhere in Albany currently. I tried New York. There were five people of that name listed in New York, but their ages were wrong.

I even did a nation-wide search. There were quite a number, fifteen or seventeen Frank Donaghys, but no-one fitted the profile. I even searched the obituaries.

Another time I searched for the last name Donaghy in Albany, with any first name, hoping to find grandparents, uncles, cousins. There were none listed.

At 18 I thought Uncle John was my best bet when it came to getting more information. But he responded to my questions in much the same way as Nana had responded on numerous occasions, as if there was an agreed upon response to my questions.

"Well, Frank took it so badly when your mother died. He needed to get away to clear his head, and then he never came back".

"Didn't anyone try to find him, to check on him?" I asked frustrated. "What about his parents? Did he have brothers and sisters?"

A small voice in my head was saying *"Didn't he ask about me? Didn't he check to be sure I was okay? Didn't he care about me?"* But I didn't say it. It was painful to put into words that he didn't care enough to come back for me.

Uncle John had answered "I don't know. We were not friendly with the Donaghy's and after your mother died, we just lost contact."

He shrugged and said not unkindly "Let it go Una. It's for the best."

I didn't let it go then. There was one more person who might tell me something – John's wife Mary. I knew John and Mary married shortly after my mother died – twenty years ago now. Mary must have met Frank Donaghy. He would still have been around at that time.

Mary looked uncomfortable when I brought up the subject on one of my weekend trips home from college. She said to talk to Uncle John.

I sensed there was something she didn't want to tell me. They were hiding something from me.   Maybe they were protecting my feelings. They didn't want to come right out and say that my father had abandoned me.

Reluctantly I put the search on the back burner while I focused on my final year of college, graduation, and my move to New York.   And then I was too busy with my life in New York to think about my father

It was probably Nana's death that brought up all these questions about my father again.   I accepted that Nana had died, and I accepted that my mother had died, but my father is alive - probably alive - somewhere. Why doesn't he want to know me?

TWENTY-ONE

Feeling slightly embarrassed at my show of self-pity, I stood up to make some toast and pour myself more coffee, determined to banish those self-pitying thoughts from my mind.

A thought struck me as I absent-mindedly munched on a piece of toast. Had Ben saved Nana's letters somewhere? Since he had saved those old photos, it was likely he had saved the letters too. But where?

But would Nana be more revealing to him in a letter than she had been to me all my life? It was anybody's guess. I was beginning to suspect that my Nana had been quite secretive. And I didn't understand why.

Maybe there would be more information about Josie and her problems.

The room I had started to call "the study" was the most likely place. I would search in there.

I did a quick search of all the likely places – desk drawers, even hidden corners of bookshelves – but found no letters. Maybe he hadn't saved them after all. Or maybe they would show up in some unlikely spot.

I picked up the black folder again, the one that had contained the old photos. I remembered there had been some typewritten pages which I had not read last night as I had become so fascinated with the old photos, and there had been other envelopes also that I hadn't opened. I had only opened the ones that said "photos" on the outside.

Now I saw there was a thin envelope tucked far down in the front pocket of the folder. I hadn't noticed it last night. When I opened it, I saw it was a letter and it was written in Nana's distinctive handwriting. Eagerly I opened it and laid the pages on the desk.

There were two and a half pages of her writing in faded blue ink on what they used to call airmail paper. They used to use it because it weighed less in that era when long letters would be written back and forth across the Atlantic, before emails existed and before phone calls were affordable. Nana still had some in her drawer in the living room - used to have some, I corrected myself, wondering sadly if Uncle John and his family had removed all of Nana's furniture from the house already.

I resolved to never visit them there. I couldn't bear to see the house transformed.

****

The letter was dated June 3, 1950.

Dear Ben,

I am sorry it has been so long since I wrote to you last. I hope Mam and Dad and yourself, are keeping well as are Josie and myself. We have been busy here but are glad to be working and making decent money. Everything is so different here and we miss home.

There is no need to apologize that you didn't give the letter to Frank. It was a whim I had to make peace with him. It was a bad idea. As you said, he is making a new life for himself, and the past should be left in the past.

I hope Dad isn't working too hard. Any news about yourself and Eileen? We have gone to a few dances here and met some fellows but nobody serious for us yet.

There was a little more to the letter, mentioning places

they had visited in New York, but no more mention of the mysterious Frank.

What did this mean? And who was Frank? Nana had written Frank a letter which she had asked Ben to pass on, but Ben hadn't done so. What did that mean? Why was she trying to make peace with him? And why didn't Ben pass it on?

My reverie was interrupted by a loud rapping on the door. I was a little startled. It was only nine o'clock. In the morning.

A quick look out the window revealed a van with "Vodaphone" written in large letters on the side.

A friendly red-haired young fellow stood on the doorstep and announced that he needed to check the wires inside for my phone and internet.

I stood aside to let him in, pleased he had come so soon. It would be much easier to communicate, especially with the U.S. with WIFI set up. I would be able to use my laptop. I would really need it to communicate with Silas as I completed by designs. The landline was included with the internet. It was "a package deal" the Vodaphone man said.

I realized I didn't know where the phone wires were inside the house, but he had already figured it out from looking at where they entered the house and made his way back through the hall to the study.

It took less than five minutes to get the connection set up, and then we both realized simultaneously that I didn't actually have a phone. The ancient phone I found on a bookshelf didn't offer a dial tone. He assured me that the wires were "sound" and worked when he tested them, and I just needed to buy a phone.

I thanked him but thought I probably didn't need a phone. My cell phone worked fine. As soon as he was gone brought my laptop down from my bedroom and set it up with the password for the internet.

The setup went smoothly, and I was able to access my email. Of course, I had been checking emails on my phone but hadn't done that this morning.

There were a few greetings from friends – Liz, Gina and Sandra, and one from Silas with an attachment. I looked quickly at the date it was sent early this morning. That was good. He had sent me details for the first set of drawings and a chapter from the book I would be illustrating.

I glanced through it briefly and planned to get to work on it a little later.

TWENTY-TWO

Now I had more impetus to investigate that cemetery – if indeed it was a cemetery. There might be headstones with the Donaghy name on them! The man in the photo was Frank Donaghy and he may or not be the same Frank mentioned in the letters. It was likely that he had lived locally, and if he had, there might still be Donaghys living locally.

Of course, that didn't mean they were related to my father. Still, it was intriguing. I knew nothing about my father, had never met another person named Donaghy, so if there were people in the vicinity with my last name, I would feel a kinship with them.

I could also ask people about Donaghys currently living in the area. Seán Clohessy would know. Liam said he was the one who knew all about Lockamore and its history.

I would be sure to drop into the pub on Sunday again when he would be there. Maybe he was there on other days too. And his daughter did give me her phone number and said to drop by. I might walk down Doone Road later, past their house.

Or maybe I should call first. I wasn't sure of the etiquette. Could I just ring their doorbell as Liam had rung mine yesterday, or should I call first?

But now I would go for a walk. I would walk down Doone Road turning left from the house and see who or what my neighbors were on that side. Was there in fact a cemetery or was my imagination overactive last night? I didn't remember seeing one when I drove by on the way to the supermarket on Sunday, but my eyes were on the road. I hadn't looked to the side. If there was, it would be a small cemetery and might not extend as far as the road. I would walk slowly and observe everything.

Now that I knew what to look for, I easily picked out the old fence that bordered my property – only it didn't extend all the way to the road in the front. There was a tall hedge that ran back about 20 feet and joined the fence back there. The hedge continued parallel to Doone Road for a few yards. There was a wire fence that continued where the hedge left off.

Not exactly neat and organized, I thought – in fact, a bit of a hodge-podge.   Nevertheless, the boundaries of my property were quite clearly marked now that I knew what to look for.

The wire fence along the side of the road was low and easy to step over too. The field inside was overgrown. A rusted gate held closed by a circle of wire over two posts, also didn't look like it would keep anyone out who had an urge to explore. Yet I hesitated. I wanted to be on good terms with neighbors and I didn't know the protocol.

I continued along Doone road and saw that there was a house that looked occupied and well cared for further along. There was a white fence that looked quite new and very noticeable, running along the front and on both sides back as far as I could see.   That household had marked its boundaries quite clearly.

I retraced my steps and stood at the rusted gate trying to see more of the property. No tombstones loomed up. Maybe I was imagining things last night. This was just an overgrown field, full of weeds.

I was so absorbed that I hadn't paid attention to the noise of the car and was startled when it zoomed past. It screeched to a stop about ten feet ahead and a white head poked out of the door on the passenger side. Seán Clohessy!

He was shouting something I couldn't hear and waving at me. I hurried up to the car, as he slowly emerged.

"Miss O'Loughlin, I see you are surveying your neighbors!"

he called out.

"And you are just the man I want to see" I called out in response. "I was trying to get an idea of the boundary of my property and wondering who owned this" nodding my head in the direction of the overgrown field.

"Hickeys used to own it" Seán answered. "They probably still do, but we haven't seen them around here in ages".

Having reached the car, I bent to wave at the driver, thinking it would be Deirdre. Instead, I saw a young dark-haired boy in a leather jacket.

"Hiya!" he said with a friendly grin. 'I'm Noel. You moved into the O'Loughlin house I take it".

"She is a returned Yank" Seán broke in. "Benjy's grand-niece home from America. And this fellow here is my grand-son".

"How are you finding it so far?" Noel asked curiously. "Is it your first time in Ireland?"

"It is and I like it, but I'm still getting used to things," I said "there was so much I don't know".

To Seán I said "Liam O'Riordan came by yesterday and he brought me to see the fields at the back. On the way back to the house through the back I thought I saw an old cemetery at the back of this field". I gestured towards the field that Seán had said belonged to Hickey.

Somewhat apologetically I added "It was getting dark, and I couldn't see that clearly, so maybe I am wrong".

"It used to be an old cemetery years ago" Noel acknowledged. "You can't see it from the road though". He looked curious. "Are there still some gravestones standing?"

"I couldn't tell from the distance" I admitted. "I was thinking of going in and taking a look but didn't know if I'd get into trouble for trespassing".

There was a loud laugh from Seán. "Not at all. Aren't you the next-door neighbor? Couldn't you just be fixing your fence on that side? Come on, I'll go in with you". He started walking back in the direction of the gate.

"Grand-da I have to go now, or I'll be late" Noel called out.

"Sure, I can walk home from here" Seán said over his shoulder as he continued walking.

"I could drive him home" I offered.

Seán seemed energetic and steady on his feet, but he must be 90, maybe older. The walking stick was nowhere in sight. I wasn't sure how much walking he usually did.

"He will be okay" Noel assured me. 'Do you have our number?"

"Yes. Your mother gave it to me the other day. I can also bring him back to my house for tea for a while" I added.

"That's grand so" Noel nodded with approval. "I have a lecture in an hour at the Uni. I'll be late if I don't leave immediately".

I waved goodbye and hurried to catch up with Seán who had reached the gate and was unhooking the wire that kept it closed. When I reached him, he nodded in the direction of the house next door with the white fence. "Did you meet the Duggans?" he asked.

"No" I answered. "I only met you and Liam O'Riordan so far, and the other people at the pub on Sunday".

"Well, they are new-comers. They are from Cork. They

bought the house and a patch of land from the Hickeys. They didn't want the whole thing. I don't know why. It wouldn't have cost much more".

Gallantly Seán held the rusted gate open for me to enter. The grass was long inside the gate, but the ground was level at this point. It rose gradually and when we walked up the slight incline, I saw that it sloped down again on the other side. And there was the graveyard! The slope of the land hid it from the road.

"I haven't been here in a long time" Seán said. "We used to come in here, Benjy and me and Mikey, when we were boys and smoke cigarettes."

He stopped and surveyed the scene. "It is a bit more run-down but hasn't really changed".

He wasn't the slightest bit winded after his quite rapid walk up the slope. I was impressed.

There were the remains of an old stone wall, crumbled in places, that might have surrounded the graves at one point, but no sign of a gate or an entrance of any type.

I could see several, about five or six, old gravestones with a Celtic cross on top, and several shorter slabs.

I thought of what he had said about sneaking in here as a boy to smoke cigarettes – that must have been more than 70 years ago!

"So, when you came here as a boy was it being used, or was it abandoned by then?" I asked.

"Oh, it was old then." He answered. "They opened the new cemetery, St. John's, out by Reagans Road...When was it?" He stared in the distance trying to remember "In the 1930s sometime. But this hadn't been used for a while before that".

He looked at me gravely. "You know who they say is buried here?" When I didn't answer he continued "The Civil War dead".

"The Civil War?" I asked stupidly, then remembered my Irish history. "Oh yes, 1921 or 1922".

"That's right". He nodded approvingly. "There was a lot of strife in these parts. You know Michael Collins was from Cork and there was a lot of support for him. But there were enough Free Staters around too. They say brothers fought against brothers. There were executions."

He nodded as he stared at the graves. I wanted to ask which side did his family take, which side did mine take?

"There are some O'Loughlins buried here" Seán was saying. "I don't remember where exactly. And some Clohessys – here is a Clohessy".

He stopped by one of the stones with a Celtic Cross and I read the faded lettering "Patrick Clohessy, 1899-1921, RIP. You died for your country".

Seán nodded as if acknowledging Patrick. "He was my father's older brother."

"He was only 22" I said sadly.

Seán was already moving along what I saw now used to be a pathway. There were bits of pavement showing under the weeds. "There was a Loughlin over here somewhere".

I glanced curiously at names on the headstones as I followed him. I stopped suddenly.

"Donaghy! Is that Donaghy?" I asked.

Seán stopped and peered at the old headstone. This was just a slab, smaller, and looked much older than many of the others. It could easily be overlooked. He moved closer so that he could read the lettering. I followed him.

"It is!" he pronounced. "Colm Donaghy". He pronounced it *Culum.*

I tried to read the inscription. Some of it was too faint to make out.

"A ways rem bered dear fa her a d husband, 185 – 19 0. Wife Mary died 1910. Son Seán died 1916."

"Are there still Donaghys living in Lockamore?" I asked hopefully.

"The Donaghys used to live over by Krumgedden" Seán answered. I don't know if these are related", nodding towards the grave-stone, "but I'd say they are. They were buried a long time before the new cemetery was opened. And there wasn't another one near, so it must be the same Donaghys".

I realized that Seán hadn't made the connection between me and the headstone. He probably forgot or didn't even pay attention to my last name when I first met him. He had grouped me with the O'Loughlins.

His next words proved to me I had guessed correctly.

"The only Donaghy I remember living around here was a fellah that used to live in your house. Oh, it was years ago even before Katey and Josie went away. He used to work for their father and was boarding with them."

Seán seemed to be talking to himself.   "What was the fellas name? Fergus? Frank? I think it was Frank. He used to help Benjy and his father in the fields."

"I have a photograph of him" I said. "I found old photos in the house. Frank Donaghy is one of the names on the back of a photo. He is with Katey and Josie in the photo".

Seán looked interested. "Oh, I would love to see it. Maybe I would remember more then."

"I can make you a cup of tea and show you the photos if you would like to come back to the house" I offered.

"Ah, a cup of tea! That's an offer I won't refuse" Seán said cheerfully.

We started to make our way back up towards the gate.

I also thought that he had clambered around enough. He showed no signs of tiring, but I didn't want to be responsible for wearing him out. It had helped tremendously to have him come with me. My uneasiness had gone, and I didn't feel the old cemetery was spooky and dangerous anymore. I could come back here on my own again to look at more of the headstones.

TWENTY-THREE

Seán announced that the kitchen looked the same as when Benjy was living here. I pulled out a chair for him at the kitchen table and invited him to sit while I put on the kettle.

I sliced some brown bread and put out some cheese and marmalade. It was only 11 o'clock. It could be a second breakfast. In any case there wasn't much else. I had eaten all the nice scones I had bought on Sunday. I would need to do some food shopping later today.

While the kettle was boiling, I went to get the photos. I brought back the envelope that had been labeled "Katey and Josie". I could show Seán the other photos later, but I didn't want too many distractions when he first saw the photo of Frank Donaghy.

Seán was buttering himself some brown bread when I returned. I put the envelope on the table and made the tea. After I brought it to the table I reached over and opened the envelope and selected out the one with Frank and the two girls to show him first.

Seán was already sipping his tea appreciatively as he said "Ah, a nice cup of tea"!

I held the photo out to him. "Here is the photo of Frank".

But he was studying the two girls apparently as he said

"They were such lovely-looking girls. Katey was a live wire – mischievous. And Josie! Poor Josie!"

I was so sick of hearing these insinuations about Josie. Why was Josie "poor Josie?"

I opened my mouth and then thought better of it. He seemed lost in his memories, talking more to himself than to me and his face had taken on a more serious, almost worried expression.

"Ah yes! That was a strange business!" he sighed. "She was crazy about him. Anyone could see it. I can see it here. It is all over her face".

I could stand it no more, so I broke in. "Do you remember him?"

"Oh, I do" Seán answered softly. "I remember him very well, a nice quiet fella. He lived in with them. He had only come for the Spring and Summer, but he had no transport, so they gave him a bed to stay during the week. Yes, he was one of the Donaghys from Krumgedden all right."

He had become very thoughtful. He looked at me as if not sure how to say what he wanted to say.

"You know, I always thought he was a decent lad. I could never believe he would do wrong. But I'm not accusing Josie of lying mind you. None of us can know what really happened."

"Nobody said anything to me" I burst out. "And I really would like to know."

I thought Seán would clam up, but he didn't.

Slowly he began. "After Frank arrived, we all noticed how Josie would moon around after him. She was young, no more than a child. And he was older than Ben and me. It seemed like childish adoration.

He seemed like a quiet respectful young fellow. He was serious. The family had little money and what he was earning would help them. There was some mention that he had a girl in Krumgedden, but I am not sure who said it.

Katey would have had more of a chance with him, I think. It was plain to see that he thought Josie was only a child. But Katey was already planning to go to the States."

"Not Josie too?" I asked.

"No, that only happened later. In fact, at the time Josie would say that she had everything she ever wanted here in Cork that she didn't need to go to the States."

I was astounded. All my life I had heard that Josie never wanted to go back to Ireland. In fact, she had said as much the day of Nana's will.

"So, what happened" I asked impatiently.

"The story is that Josie came running back to the house with a torn dress and crying her eyes out and said that Frank had interfered with her".

"Interfered with her?" I repeated dully, but already I was remembering that Nana would use that expression occasionally. It meant unwelcome advances, hinted at molestation. Of course, it was vague enough to make it unclear what in fact had happened. It was all dark insinuation.

"I thought it happened in the field where Frank was working" Seán continued. "Josie was crying and upset. She kept saying he disrespected her. All I know was that her mother and father and Katey were shocked and turned completely against him."

"And Benjy", I asked. "What did he think?"

"Well Benjy and Frank were close. They were good friends. Benjy had trouble believing it, but he was powerless to stop the others. The father made Frank leave immediately which he did. I heard later that he went to England.

But it was after that that Josie became even worse. She was always high-strung but now she looked a bit mad. She acted like Frank had abandoned her. Some of us began to think that maybe there was a child involved, that she was pregnant".

He looked at me "though you understand there was no sign of that. It was more the way she was talking."

"Benjy even said to me once that she was mad because Frank rejected her, that he would be surprised if Frank ever even touched her. Mind you, he said that to me, but I don't think he said that at home. But he did know Frank well. They shared a bedroom, and Frank had told him about his ambitions to buy a farm someday."

My head was reeling. Could Josie have been pregnant? Is that why she left with Nana for the U.S.? Or was Ben right, that Frank was never interested in Josie, and she accused him in anger because she felt rejected? Had she destroyed his reputation so that he felt he had to go away to England?

Seán was continuing "Josie seemed to be getting stranger in her behavior as the summer progressed. And the next thing we heard was that she was going to the States with Katey, that a job had been found for her. But even the night of the party to send them off she wasn't herself. You couldn't talk to her. She was off in her own little world. She showed no enthusiasm about going away, no sadness about leaving us".

"That's how she always seemed to me" I said as I poured more tea for Seán. I mean, strange and disconnected – in her own world".

He had been generous with his information so I should do the same.

"I didn't understand why she had no interest in coming back here or in owning the house. Even the day of Nana's will when I asked her about Lockamore she said something about it being an awful place – but she or Nana – no-one ever told me the story. Thanks for doing that."

"Katey would know the reason all right but would feel it wasn't her place to talk about Josie's experience" Seán offered. "She was always a silent one. You could never get her to tell you anything she didn't want to talk about".

"Do you know what happened to Frank Donaghy?" I asked. "Did he ever come back from England?"

"I don't know" Seán admitted. "It was a sore topic in this house, and it was hard on Benjy, so I didn't bring it up. Not that they would know anyway. But as time passed his reputation became worse with the parents. He was blamed for them losing Josie. They believed she would still be here with them if he had been a gentleman as they put it."

"It is a strange story" I said, "but even stranger is that my own father's name is Frank Donaghy".

Seán looked sharply at me. He had forgotten, or maybe never even registered my last name.

"Your mother married a Donaghy?" he asked in bafflement. "Katey's daughter? But Katey was so against him."

"You see I don't think they could be the same Donaghys", I said although I was beginning to wonder now if there was a connection. Maybe that was wishful thinking on my part.

I continued "At least it would be a great coincidence. My mother and father met when they were in school in Albany. They were the same age, or I think they were. But my mother died when I was a child, and I was raised by Nana -Katey. She would never tell me anything about the Donaghys. My father left shortly after my mother died and I could never find any information about him or his family. I knew they were of Irish background but didn't even know where in Ireland they were from, or how long ago the family had left."

Seán was looking at me with a mixture of concern and interest. "Isn't it strange that she wouldn't tell you anything about your father's family? If there was nothing to hide, she would have told you where they were from. That's what I think anyway. She didn't want to share you with them."

He stared into space. "Well, stranger things have happened" he said. "I am sure there are Donaghys still in Krumgedden and it wouldn't be hard to find out if they have people in the States, and if so where in the States. I have a feeling that Frank might have emigrated to the States, but I might have it mixed up with England. It is so long ago."

I felt such relief that Seán, unlike my family, was answering my questions and even encouraging me to investigate. I also felt a surge of gratitude.

I showed him the other photos from the envelope.

"I can see the resemblance" he said as he studied the photo of my mother. I was pleased that he thought I resembled her, though I didn't see it myself.

When he saw the photo of the four young girls he laughed, amused. He confirmed that the two girls in the hair bands were Katey and Josie and announced that the other two were Maura Lafferty and Julia Reilly. It seems Maura had married a Dublin lad and lived there now but Julia was now Julia Flynn and lived on the other side of Lockamore.

"She would love to see this" Seán laughed.

When we were finished, I offered to drive Seán home. He protested, saying it was only down the road, but I said I had to go shopping anyway so I could drop him off on the way. To that he agreed with promises that he would "drop in again for a cup of tea".

TWENTY-FOUR

Of course, the supermarket and the village of Lockamore were in the opposite direction to the Clohessy house and I hadn't really planned to go to there immediately, but after Seán had seated himself in the car and I was driving out of my driveway it made perfect sense to continue to the supermarket and mall after I had dropped him off. I might as well pick up a phone for the newly connected landline as well as some food.

But my mind was churning with the information Seán had given me about Frank Donaghy. And about Nana's stance, which I could only guess at of course, but I knew her well.

Nana would have known a lot of people in Albany and especially those who were from Ireland, and who belonged to her parish of St. Agnes.

All I knew about my father was that he and my mother had met when she was at school at St. Agnes, but ten years ago I couldn't find a record of attendance for either of them.   I believed she had been a student there because Uncle John and his three sons all had attended St Agnes.   And I course, so did I.

So, I had concluded it was almost certain they met at school. But it is unlikely I had been told that because they had told me nothing, so I had just assumed that was how it happened

At some point after they met, wherever they met, Nana would have heard Frank's last name, might have met him. Now, knowing about the older Frank Donaghy and the incident before Nana and Josie left Lockamore, I can imagine Nana's shock when she heard that her daughter was dating Frank Donaghy. It wasn't just a Donaghy, but someone with the very same first and last names as the infamous scoundrel (in her eyes) who had molested her sister all those years ago.

Of course, the name would have meant something, and of course Nana would have investigated further, tried to find out who this Frank Donaghy's family was and if he was related to the Frank they had known in the past.

Knowing Nana, she would have done that when she first discovered Annie and Frank were dating. I can't imagine her doing anything else. Would she have warned Annie about Frank, even forbidden her to continue seeing him?

I wasn't sure about that. Nana had been very benign and accepting about my boyfriends, but then I only brought home those she would find acceptable. And after all, this Frank couldn't be blamed for the behavior of the older Frank all those years before. Nana would surely see that.

But she would certainly have investigated further when Annie and Frank were talking about getting married.

Had she still believed after all those years that the older Frank had molested her sister? Or, as she saw Josie's strangeness increasing, did she ever suspect, as Benjy had, that the molestation was all in Josie's imagination? I didn't know.

I hadn't told Seán about her letter to Benjy where she had tried to get him to forward a letter to Frank. Now I wondered if it was a letter of apology. Maybe she had changed her view about what had happened.

It didn't explain why she would be opposed to my mother and father getting married - if she had been opposed, that is. I didn't know that. Again, no one in my family had ever even hinted at that. But I could understand that she would be very curious about this young man named Frank Donaghy that her daughter was marrying.

Surely that wouldn't be reason enough to oppose the

marriage! Even if she fully believed the molestation had happened would that be enough reason to hold a grudge against another young boy of the same name, whether or not he was related?

I was flummoxed! If I had been asked yesterday, even this morning, I would have said I knew Nana very well, could predict her reaction to all kinds of events. Now I wasn't so sure. She had hidden so much from me – lied by omission really.

She had never told me the story of Josie and Frank Donaghy or why Josie had such negative associations to Lockamore. I could even excuse that as she might have felt that was Josie's story to tell and not hers.

But she had kept no photograph of my mother – her only daughter – or of my father. There were no wedding photos, no photos of me as a baby. She was vague about the cause of my mother's death and the reasons for my father leaving. She "knew nothing" about my father's family or where they lived.

I accepted all of this as a child, but now it seemed increasingly unlikely that she really knew nothing about my father' family. Wouldn't they have met at the wedding? They must have lived in Albany and probably close to St. Agnes School when my father was a student there. Someone in the parish would have known them. That priest Nana was so fond of, Father Ted Johnson, he might have known them.

Of course, Nana's reluctance to talk to me about the Donaghys didn't mean necessarily that I was related to the infamous Frank. It might be that the very name caused unpleasant memories. And yet she had not tried to change my name.

I had already reached the parking lot for the supermarket. It was quite a bit fuller than it had been last Sunday morning, but I still found a space quite easily.As I walked into the mall it all seemed so familiar and I found it hard to believe that only a few days ago I had come here for the first time feeling very much a stranger and unsure of what to expect.

This time I confidently walked into Hamptons, the store with all the houseware and gadgets, where I had bought the coffee-pot. I browsed a bit and eventually approached the friendly salesgirl who said they didn't carry phones at all. She seemed genuinely sorry about this and volunteered the name of a place in Cork if I ever was there that had a good variety and good prices too.

Then chattily she enquired "Have you been here long?"

She had obviously noticed my accent and was curious.

"I have only been here a few days, but I will be here for three months at least this time' I said.

"I will drive into Cork some time, but I am just getting used to driving here so I am just driving around locally now".

She proceeded to tell me the best route to take to Cork City Centre and where to park so that I wouldn't have to deal with much traffic.

"It is better just to leave the car there and walk around, especially if you don't know the streets very well. If you drive in really early in the morning, especially on a weekend – leave here about seven – you shouldn't have much traffic" she assured me.

I thanked her and said, "I am sure I will see you again", then added impulsively "My name is Una".

She smiled and said, "Pleased to meet you Una, my name is Dymphna and I'm usually here on weekdays. See ya!"

She wasn't much younger than me I guessed.

I was in the supermarket busily perusing the different

brands of tea when my cell phone rang. It was Fergal.

"Hiya Una! How's it going?" he asked cheerfully.

"Great!" I answered. "I am definitely making myself at home".

"I wanted to ask you would you like to meet some people this week-end? Not in Cork, but in Krumgedden?"

"In Krumgedden?" I echoed bewildered. How did he know?

But he was continuing, "You probably don't remember, but the other day I told you that I am from Krumgedden. So, I am going home for the weekend. It's my father's birthday on Friday and we have a family gathering. But on Saturday I'll meet up with some friends around there, and my sister will be down from Dublin. I thought you might like to meet people our age"

"That sounds great" I managed to say, while still processing that he was from Krumgedden and I would have a great reason to go there.

"I could pick you up so you wouldn't have to drive" he offered.

"Isn't it a long way for you to come?" I asked in protest.

"It is about a half-hour" he answered. "If you were more used to the area and to driving these roads, I would say you could drive yourself, but there will be time enough for that and I don't mind picking you up. And if you wanted to stay overnight there's plenty of room at my parent's house and I could drive you back the next day".

I was about to protest that I could manage a half-hour

drive but then thought if I stayed overnight, I would probably meet his parents and other people, and since my last name was Donaghy surely someone would mention Donaghys in the area and wonder if I was related. The older people would be more knowledgeable about that.

I said, "That all sounds great."

Fergal said "How about seven on Saturday? I'll pick you up then?"

I agreed, thinking this is not a date, just a friendly invitation to meet people. But I was pleased on many levels with this invitation.

TWENTY-FIVE

I worked on my drawings for the book project over the next couple of days. I had three sketches I liked by the end of Friday, but I wanted to give myself a day or two to put some finishing touches before I sent copies to Silas. If I scanned and sent them on Sunday night, he would have them by Monday, still days before the deadline.

On Friday morning Seán's daughter Deirdre called and invited me for dinner that night.

"It will be just a family dinner, nothing fancy. My son Noel will be down from Cork. I know you already met him, and my daughter will be here too, and of course Dad and my husband. It will be a chance to have a chat."

"That sounds lovely" I said. And it did. Deirdre seemed friendly and unpretentious, and I enjoyed talking to Seán. Noel had seemed pleasant and low-key. Besides I was starting to feel very solitary. It would be nice to be in a group of people.

I didn't know how much Seán had said about our visit to the old graveyard and our conversation over tea later. I imagined nothing was kept secret. That suited me fine. I was tired of family secrets.

I was invited for 6:30. It was raining and that meant I would take the car. Walking back home on such a quiet road later tonight would not be a good idea anyway, even without rain. It would be so dark.

I wasn't used to how dark it was here at night. With no streetlights and houses few and far between to shed a little light through their windows it was darker than any other places I had lived.

I parked in their driveway behind a maroon sedan and saw I would have to back out when I left. There wasn't much space left in the driveway. Mine was the third car. Deirdre's white van was also there.

As I brought the car to a halt the front door opened, and Noel stood there waving.

"Hello! Sorry, there is so little space. My sister is here too".

I had found a bottle of whiskey in the pantry. Of course, it could have been there for years, but I grabbed it before leaving as I felt a need to bring something to the dinner. This I thrust somewhat awkwardly into Noel's hands as soon as I reached the door.

I was soon surrounded by people. A large burly man I guessed to be Deirdre's husband took the bottle from Noel with a wink saying, "I will take that from you" and then to me "There was no need. Come in. Come in!"

He stuck out his hand saying "I am Noel senior. Pleased to meet you".

We were in a warm sitting room with a fire blazing. It looked cozy. Seán was sitting in an armchair by the fire and a pretty, blond girl was standing next to him looking curiously at me.

She walked over and said "Una, I am Lina. Pleased to meet you."

Then to her father and brother. "Ye are so delighted with the whiskey you didn't even take the woman's coat".

Then to me "Here Una, give it to me and I'll hang it up for you".

Deirdre shouted from the kitchen in the back. "I'll be out in a minute Una. I'm just sticking something in the oven".

Seán waved for me to come and sit by him, and I did and was soon joined by the others.

Noel Senior said "So, how are you surviving your first week in Ireland?"

"It's hard to believe it's not even a week yet" I replied. "Of course, everything is different, but I already feel quite at home".

"I think it is an amazing story" Lina chimed in. "I mean to have inherited a house and to never have been here. Did you know anything about the place at all beforehand?"

"Not a thing" I said. "I knew my Nana grew up here in Lockamore with her brother Ben and sister Josie. She never mentioned to me that Ben had died and that she inherited the house. Then of course she was sick for a while. She died this summer and the first time I heard about the house was at the reading of her will".

Lina wanted to know if I had brothers and sisters.

"No" I said "but I have three first cousins. My grandmother had only two children, my mother who died and my uncle John, who has three sons".

I added quickly before they tried to find a tactful way to ask.

"She left her house in Albany to my uncle John, so they are moving in there. She said she knew that John wasn't so interested in Ireland, but she believed I was and would be – and" I laughed, "she was right. So, everyone in the family is happy with the arrangement". I wasn't completely happy of course, but I didn't need to share that with this nice welcoming family.

"But it must be an adjustment" Lina persisted "to be in a small country village in Ireland after living in a city in the United States. Is Albany a big city?"

"It is big enough" I answered. "That is where I grew up. But I was living in New York before I left".

That brought fresh exclamations of "She moved from New York to Lockamore!".

At that point Deirdre emerged from the kitchen and gave me a welcoming hug.

"I'm glad you came" she said beaming, "and I see you are being peppered with questions from my nosey family".

"Oh, sure we're only making her feel at home" Lina protested.

Deirdre said to me. "I'm cooking roast chicken and potatoes. It is almost ready."

I nodded vigorously. "That sounds great".

"These two are not living at home so I don't see them that often" Deirdre said, nodding in the direction of her two children. Lina is working in Limerick and of course Noel is at the university in Cork."

"I am a secondary school teacher" Lina volunteered. "I teach French and Spanish".

"I would love to speak another language" I said. "And of course, now, seeing signs written in Irish, I wish I could read some".

"It's not an easy language if you didn't grow up with it" Noel senior said. "Seán here is quite fluent, but he doesn't use it much these days".

"Ah ná bac leis" Seán said.

Everyone seemed to understand so I didn't like to ask what he had said, assuming it was an Irish/Gaeilic expression.

Noel, however, said "he is saying don't bother with it. He is being modest."

"I'd love to learn a few words and phrases some time Seán" I said "If you have the time and patience to teach me."

"You can make me a cup of tea some day and some of that nice brown bread and we'll see" Seán said, but he looked pleased.

"Well, I think it is time to sit down to eat" Deirdre said, getting up. "Lina and Noel come out with me and help me put the food on the table".

The dining table was in a separate room, adjoined to the kitchen, but with a large archway separating them. Noel senior pulled out a chair for me saying "Why don't you sit here Una," as Seán moved to sit opposite me in what I assumed was his usual place.

The food was hot, plentiful, and delicious. Everyone ate appreciatively and silently for a few minutes. Then Seán said

"Una showed me old photos that Benjy had in the house. There was one of Julia Flynn as a girl with Katey and Josie".

"She would like to see that" Deirdre said. "Julia was always one for old photos. And of course, she would love to meet you Una, and to talk about Katey and the old days".

Seán nodded assent. "You might see her around. She is living on the other side of the village."

"We will introduce you" Deirdre said.

Seán asked, "Are there Donaghys still living over in Krumgedden?"

"There's a Joe Donaghy from around there" Noel senior answered. "Why are you asking?"

"When I was a lad there was a Frank Donaghy who used to help out at the O'Loughlins. He was from Krumgedden. Una had a photo of him she found with all the old photos. I thought he went to England, but there was a big family of them there."

Seán seemed about to say more but then paused.

"I'd say Joe Donaghy is in his 50's" Noel senior answered, "so he might be a son or a nephew".

I said "My last name is Donaghy of course, but I don't know where my father's family came from. I was curious about the name and wondering if he might be related to them."As I spoke, I realized it must sound like such a long shot to them.

It was clear that none of the others knew the story of Josie and Frank Donaghy. They were more focused on establishing that my father had been born in the United States and that the family didn't know where in Ireland they had come from. They accepted that as not unusual for "Yanks" who had lost track of their ancestry.

"Well, I suppose anything is possible" Deirdre said. "If you met any of the Donaghys over there you could find out if they had anyone who had emigrated to the States".

Seán looked interested. "And you could find out what happened to Frank Donaghy. Did he indeed go to England, or was it America and if so, did he come back? I know he wasn't around for a while – not around here anyway."

I told them that I had been invited to Krumgedden to a party. There were comments of approval that I was getting a chance to get out and about and getting to know people. Noel Junior said he knew Fergal Sullivan slightly and knew his younger sister a bit better.

We had tea and a delicious pavlova for dessert. I started to help with clearing dishes but was firmly told to sit down by the fire and have another cup of tea. I was joined by Seán. Presently "young Noel" appeared from upstairs where he had disappeared briefly.

"I did a quick search online for Frank Donaghy born around 1935 in Krumgedden" he said, and I found one, born in 1930. That would make him about 4 years older than you Grand-da. He must be the one".

Seán and I expressed amazement at his enterprise and speed.

"Here's the interesting thing" Noel continued. "Frank Donaghy emigrated to the States in 1953."

Seán and I looked at each other in surprise. Seán said "that would be a few years after Katey and Josie left. I think they left around 1950. I really thought he went to England before they went away".

"He might have" Noel answered. "That wouldn't show up in the records. He could have gone over to England and come back and emigrated to the States from here. He left from Cobh".

I knew Cobh was in Cork and a major departure point for emigrant ships in the past. Katey and Josie had sailed from Cobh to New York.

"He sailed with his wife Eileen and son aged two or three. I forget his name" Noel said apologetically, "but I wrote down the web address so you could look yourself". He handed the piece of paper to me.

I thanked him profusely and said, "Years ago I tried to get information about my father and none of this showed up in my searches". I was feeling a bit foolish that I hadn't thought to do a search myself.

"You probably wouldn't have found the information then. Fairly recently the Irish Government made all kinds of information available from records. You should have another look now" Noel said.

I was about to say that I had been looking for records of my father's birth in Albany but then thought that was almost eight years ago. I hadn't looked since then. There were probably all kinds of records available now that were not available then.

But Seán had grasped the significance of the older Frank Donaghy emigrating to the United States.

"You should look into that, Una" he said. "He might even be your grandfather".

My mind was reeling. "Wouldn't that be strange!" I said.

What I didn't say was where is my father? Why did he disappear?

TWENTY-SIX

After getting home from the Clohessys I immediately went to my laptop and found the website Noel had written down.   I quickly found the information Noel had already given me.

Frank Donaghy (23), wife Eileen (23), and son Tadhg (2) from Krumgedden, Cork had left Cobh on July 19, 1953, on the Caledonia, bound for New York.

Based on Benjy's letters to Nana, I knew that in 1953 Nana and Josie were living in New York City. Nana and Grand-da had moved to Albany around 1955.

What were the chances that Frank Donaghy, and family had also moved to Albany? Probably it was too much of a coincidence, but then again, why did Nana, a usually sociable woman, know nothing about my father's family? And what had happened to my father?

I did a search for Frank Donaghy, born in 1966 in Albany, NY, and as I expected, there were no results. That is what had happened years ago when I had tried to find my father.

Frustrated, I typed in "Tadhg Donaghy" and again came up with nothing. Tadhg had been 2 in 1953. He couldn't have just disappeared. Even if he had died there should be a record somewhere.

Then on a hunch I typed in "Tim" and "Timothy", the English versions of Tadhg – and bingo! I found Timothy Donaghy living in Albany in 1965 and playing with the St. Agnes Bulls – the school football team - the school I had also attended. Timothy would have been 15.

Fascinated, I searched the St. Agnes yearbook page for 1967, two years later. Timothy wasn't listed. I searched for the following year, still no Timothy. Had he dropped out? Had he graduated and not been listed in the yearbook for some reason that I couldn't think of?

He was Frank Donaghy's son. Or was he? He was the same age as Tadhg would have been and Timothy was the English version of Tadhg. It was possible but I couldn't be certain. I closed the laptop and went to bed.

I woke early the next morning and lay in bed thinking of how friendly and welcoming Seán and his family had been. Noel had found that information about the elder Frank Donaghy very quickly. Maybe he would help me do more searching. I wasn't having much luck on my own.

Then as I stared at the ornate white molding on the wall just below the ceiling, which reminded me of the icing on a wedding cake, I thought "My parent's wedding!" Surely the Donaghy's – my father's family – would have been at their son's wedding.

I had been so focused on looking up birth records I hadn't thought of marriage records – or death records for that matter. There must be an obituary for my mother.

I started with obituaries, bringing my coffee into the study, and sitting at the desk, laptop open. But there was nothing. There was no official death record, no obituary in the local Albany papers – not that I could access online anyway.

I moved on to marriages. I started with 1985. They would have been 19. They had met in High School. They probably married young. There was nothing for 1985 – the year I was born. No one had told me this, but I had long assumed they married because my mother was pregnant with me.

I searched 1984 next, and at last I found something:

Frank Donaghy, 18 of Saranac Lake, and Annie O'Loughlin, 18 of Albany were married on June 20 at a Civil Ceremony at the Watkins Glen Freedom Community.

The source was the Adirondack Informer. Two facts struck me simultaneously. Saranac Lake was in the Adirondacks, and they were not married in a Catholic church.

That was closely followed by a third realization –they might have eloped, and if so, their families were not present.   I had never heard of the Watkins Glen Freedom Community. It sounded like some sort of alternative community – a commune!

If my parents were living in a commune, were they hippies? Or did they simply pick this place for their marriage because they knew that their families would not get along?   I couldn't imagine Nana approving of this wedding, but of course I knew nothing about my father's family.

I couldn't answer those questions now, but I did have new information. My father was from Saranac Lake, not Albany. I knew where it was. I had even been there a few times.

I could look for birth records for my father in Saranac Lake – and for the elder Frank Donaghy. Maybe this is where they had lived – still lived. It would explain why I could never find them in Albany.

Why had I believed my parents met at St. Agnes High School? Had someone told me? Or had I just assumed that? I didn't know.

I entered "Donaghy" into the search box, and "Saranac Lake". This time I got a string of responses.

Frank, Eileen, and Timothy Donaghy were listed as residents of Saranac Lake in 1968. This was courtesy of the white pages. Frank was listed as about 40, Eileen 35-40, and Timothy

17. Those were the right ages for the family that had emigrated from Krumgedden in 1953.

But I didn't see a listing for my father, who would have been 2 years old then. He had to be from the same family.

Idly, I searched for the nearest high school to Saranac Lake and then in the yearbook for graduating seniors. There was Timothy Donaghy, a smiling good-looking dark-haired young man. Had the family relocated from Albany somewhere after 1965?

I almost missed it – a reference to a newspaper article in the Saranac Post in 1974 that mentioned Frank Donaghy.

"The annual Christmas Festival was well attended. The appearance of Santa who skied into town behind a chariot laden with gifts was a big hit with the local children. Jon Winthrop aged 7 and Frank Donaghy aged 8 both agreed it was the best Festival ever."

That was my father! It had to be! But there was still no connection to the elder Frank Donaghy or to Tadhg.

But I was getting someplace. Next, I searched the Saranac High School's graduating senior yearbook for 1983. My luck held out. There was Frank Donaghy!

I stared at the picture, aware that this was the first picture of my father I had ever seen. He was handsome, dark-haired, looked like Timothy, but his was a serious face. He was not smiling. The caption underneath said "Frank, our creative genius, voted most likely to become a mad artist".

My father was an artist! This was something we had in common, something I might have inherited from him. I felt cheated. Why had no-one told me. I felt angry with Nana and with Uncle John. Why had they deprived me of any knowledge about my father?

And no-one had said he had died. Was he alive somewhere? Where was he?

He didn't attend St. Agnes High School after all. And what about my mother? I thought she had, but there was no record of her graduation. Where had they met? And what was this place where they got married?

I looked next for listings for Watkins Glen Freedom Community. There were no phone listings. I searched on Wikipedia without holding up much hope. But I found something.

Watkins Glen Freedom Community was a community organization started in 1968 by Cedric Monkhouse, a self-professed spiritual leader. It claimed to free people from the restrictions placed on them by society by providing free living accommodations and food, as well as a spiritual experience involving a combination of yoga, meditation, and freedom to express creativity. It attracted young artists in the early 1970s and became known as an artist's community. In 2000 a series of scandals led to the eventual closing of the community.

There were claims that Cedric Monkhouse had encouraged experimentation with drugs, particularly LSD, as a pathway to enlightenment. In addition, there was also a distrust of conventional medicine and members were encouraged to use natural herbal treatments. It was claimed that this combination led to the untimely deaths of two young women due to lack of treatment. Gillian Fenster aged 23, suffered complications from untreated diabetes, and Annie Donaghy, aged 34, had complications related to pregnancy.

I stared in shock at the screen. I had wanted to know about my parents. Now that I did it was too much. Part of me didn't want to know any more.

Had my mother been a drug addict? My father too? Is this

what Nana didn't want me to know?

****

My phone was buzzing persistently intruding on my thoughts.   It was Fergal wanting to arrange a time to pick me up. Could we meet earlier than 7?

We arranged for 5:30, earlier than I had anticipated, so after hanging up I started to get ready, still in a daze. I needed to pack a change of clothes and more importantly, pick out something appropriate to wear tonight.

I would have to leave the investigation into my parents for another time. In a way that was a relief. What I was discovering was hard to process.

TWENTY-SEVEN

Fergal hugged me enthusiastically and seemed happy to see me. He looked even more handsome than I remembered. I still didn't know if this was a date or if he was simply introducing one of his uncle's clients to family and friends. Or just being kind-hearted to a solitary stranger.

In the car he explained again that we had been invited to a party at a neighbor's house and that later we would all go for drinks to the pub we were originally intending to visit, where we would meet more people, including his parents. There had been a small father gathering yesterday for his father's birthday and there would be a celebration with friends this evening. His father didn't want a fuss made for his birthday, so they had compromised by having the pub gathering.

The party was a 21st birthday party for a neighbor, Orla Ryan, and I wondered briefly why we were attending a party for 21-year-olds. I was sure that Fergal was a few years older than me, and at 24 I felt too mature for a 21st birthday party.

However, as soon as we pulled up outside the house and parked behind many cars, I saw people of all ages going into the house. When we got inside this was even more true. There were elderly people sitting around a large room, there were children running around in another room, as well as a collection of friends of Orla, a petite blond girl, who greeted us enthusiastically.

I realized the entire neighborhood had been invited to the party. There was food laid out buffet style on a large, long table, and people were milling around talking and eating.

Fergal seemed to know everyone and introduced me many

times. I gave up on trying to remember names. They all greeted me by name, however. Fergal said they all knew each other and only had to remember one new name, but I had a much more difficult problem.

I met his parents. His father, Matt's brother, looked like Matt. His mother had the same blue eyes as Fergal. They seemed to know my story. There was much oohing and aahing about how I had inherited Uncle Ben's house.

At one point I mentioned to Fergal's mother in what I hoped was a polite tone that my last name was Donaghy not O'Loughlin as she had introduced me as "the O'Loughlin girl from Lockamore" to several people.

After today's discovery I wasn't so sure anymore that I wanted to pursue the Donaghy connection in Krumgedden – if there was one – but since I was here, I felt compelled to at least mention my name.

I didn't think she paid attention or maybe didn't hear me due to the increasing volume of voices until she appeared by my side a few minutes later with an older man in tow.

"Una, I would like you to meet another Donaghy. This is Seán Donaghy".

The man shook hands with me quite formally. He looked to be in his fifties.

"Hello Una and welcome. I hear you just arrived from America."

I nodded in agreement, suddenly at a loss for words.

He continued "Some of my family are in New York."

I found my voice. "My father's name was Frank Donaghy", I said.

"And whereabouts was he from?" Seán asked.

"I don't know" I admitted. "I lost my parents when I was very young and was raised by my grandmother."

That was true. I didn't add that my father was alive as far as I knew.

"And your mother was related to Ben Loughlin?" Seán continued. I couldn't quite read the expression in his eyes, but he was making some connection.

"Yes, my grandmother was Katey O'Loughlin, and she was Ben's sister" I answered.

"Ah, yes, Katey," he responded thoughtfully.

"Did you know her?" I asked.

Even as I said it, I realized that was unlikely. Nana had never come back to Ireland and this man Seán would not have been born before she left.

"I heard of her" Seán said. "My uncle, Frank, used to work at their farm when he was young. He was friends with Ben, and he knew the sisters too."

"It is a small world" I answered, not sure if I should say that I knew some of the story.

It was sinking in that Frank from that old photo was this man's uncle - the same Frank Josie had been infatuated with and had accused of molesting her. I wondered if Seán knew the story. Of course, he did. I was learning quickly there were no secrets here.

I was trying to think of how I would ask the next question when he said,

"Frank emigrated too and lived in New York for years. His son Tadhg came back recently and is thinking of settling down here when he retires."

My mouth fell open. Tadhg could be my uncle or grandfather.

Seán was continuing obliviously. "So, the two of you would have something in common. Are you planning to stay too now that you have a house?"

I managed to stutter that I was here for three months, and then had to take care of things in New York, and then hoped to return – the response I had now given to several people.

I then added, "Yes it would be great to talk to someone else from New York who is intending to make the move back here."

"I don't know when he will arrive, but he is trying to buy a house here. He is close to retiring" Seán said. "He'd be close to 60 now. He wants to start looking for a house now before retiring."

Hardly daring to breathe I asked, "Would his family be coming too?"

"His wife, yes, but I don't think his children would come. They have never been here and of course they are all working in the States. I don't think the son Frank has much interest. The others might. I don't know." A look of derision crossed his face as he said, "The son even changed his name".

"Oh? Why? What to?" I was holding my breath.

"It was something beginning with D, so he kept that at least – Dillon, was it? Or Dinsmore – yes, that's it – Frank Dinsmore, the artist. He cut himself off from his whole family from what I hear".

"That seems cold". I gasped. "What would make him do that?"

"It happened years ago. I don't know the whole story, but he was married when he was very young, and the wife died. Somehow, he blamed his family. There was a young child too. I don't know what happened to her."

Fergal appeared out of nowhere, throwing his arm around my shoulder and talking loudly.

"Seán! How are ya! I see you met our Yank – another Donaghy too!"

"Fergal! Grand to see you! I was telling Una here about Tadhg. Maybe she can meet him when he comes back. They can compare notes about settling down here".

Fergal looked at me, pleased. "That would be great. We want Una to feel at home, so she'll stay."

"I am delighted to meet so many people" I managed to stutter. My mind was reeling.

I had a name for my father! I even thought I knew who he was. I had heard of Frank Dinsmore. He was a well-regarded New York artist.

Fergal was saying, "If you are ready, we could start making our way down to McCanns."

I nodded in agreement.

Seán was still standing there, so I said tentatively

"I could give you my cell phone number, so you could be in touch or if Tadhg would want to be in touch."

We exchanged numbers. I had made the first connection to my father's family.

TWENTY-EIGHT

I was ready to go home that night, but it was late when we finally left the pub and Fergal assumed I was staying over, so I did.

The evening had passed in a haze of faces and introductions and shouted conversations. There was no opportunity to tell Fergal what I had discovered. I wasn't sure I would have anyway. I wasn't sure I was ready to share this with anyone. It felt too raw, the sense of rejection, of abandonment.

He had changed his name. He didn't want to be found. He didn't want me in his life. Frank Dinsmore had been hiding in plain sight all this time.

Later, in bed in the O'Sullivan's small guestroom, it occurred to me that my father hadn't hidden his new name from his family. If Seán knew it, then his extended family in Krumgedden knew it. I wondered if Nana had known too, and how to reach him. Maybe she had even tried, and when he didn't respond had told me nothing to protect me. Still, I was not happy with her or with Uncle John or with Mary. I had a right to know, especially when I became an adult.

I slept soundly despite my mental turmoil, and in the morning awoke to a subdued clatter in the kitchen and the smell of bacon. I pulled on some clothes and made my way to the bathroom where I washed my face and combed my hair. I could take a shower when I got home. I was glad I had brought a change of clothes, a casual sweatshirt, which I pulled on and my jeans, and hesitantly made my way in the direction of the kitchen.

Mrs. O'Sullivan – Nora - was sitting at the kitchen table drinking tea, and Sorla, Fergal's sister, was at the stove.

Sorla had been friendly last night but there hadn't been

much chance for conversation.   Now she looked up smiling.

"Ah, Una, you are awake! Did you sleep okay?"

She was dressed in a white terry-cloth robe, her blond hair tousled.

"I am making scrambled eggs. Would you like some?"

"I don't want to take your breakfast" I muttered.

"Oh, I made loads" she answered cheerfully. "I know there will be some ravenous men in the kitchen shortly".

Nora was pulling out a chair for me at the table and saying "Here, sit down Una. Would you prefer coffee?"

I said, "tea would be fine thanks" eyeing the teapot on the table, "and yes Sorla, I'll have some eggs too if there is enough".

I sat down as Nora poured tea for me into a large blue mug. Within minutes Sorla had placed a plate of scrambled eggs and toast in front of me and had seated herself opposite me with her own plate.

Her mother was eating cereal. The atmosphere was friendly and low-key. I felt comfortable. Sorla was filling in her mother on the events of the evening, people she had seen. I thought how wonderful it would be to grow up in a family like this.

Eventually Nora turned to me and asked "How did you find it, Una? Did you enjoy yourself?"

I agreed that everyone was very friendly and welcoming, but it was hard to remember names.

"There was Seán Donaghy of course. You will remember him" Nora said, and then to Sorla,

"Seán's cousin from America wants to move back here. He

wants to buy a house."

"Where are your father's people from Una?" Sorla asked.

"I don't know. I was only four when my mother died, and I don't know what happened to my father."

If they were curious about my father they didn't say so. Instead, Nora said thoughtfully "Yes, your grandmother was Katey O'Loughlin, Ben's sister."

I might have told them then what I had learned from talking to Seán Donaghy. I felt so accepted and safe sitting at that kitchen table.

"Seán Donaghy told me ...." I started to say, when Fergal silently appeared in the kitchen doorway looking sleepy and unshaven, wearing a long-sleeved grey tee-shirt, sweatpants and barefoot. He looked adorable.

He had sat by me last night, put his arm around me as we walked to the car, and there had been no mention of a girlfriend. But he had also not given any indication that he was interested in me other than as a friend. I tried not to stare as he boiled water and took out a jar of instant coffee.

Nora was asking me how I like being in Ireland so far.

"I really like it.   It is very different of course" I answered, "but people have been so helpful."

"Una is an artist" Fergal announced as he took a seat at the table.

That led to more questions, and I explained that I was working on illustrations for a children's book. Fergal had not heard the details of this and appeared interested in hearing more about the project. That led to a description of my art classes and my life in New York.

"Would you give up all that to live here?" Sorla asked incredulously. "I mean, I love coming back and seeing everyone, but I like living in Dublin. It is very quiet around here, especially for a young person."

Her honesty prompted more than the stock response from me.

"It all happened so quickly. I only discovered in September that this house existed and that I owned it" I admitted. "Because I was between jobs, I was able to come for three months and do my free-lance work from here. I want to keep the house. It was important to Ben that it stay in the family, and besides I do really like it here. But I do have an apartment in New York, and friends."

I knew I was talking fast but I continued. "I don't know. My Nana died in July, and she raised me. The house here is a connection to her too, but I don't know how I will handle everything".

"And you are so young so have such responsibility and to be so alone" Nora said sympathetically.

My eyes started to fill up at her kind tone and I bent my head over my tea hoping no one noticed.

Fergal said "And you have only been here a week. You need time to figure things out."

"Yes", Nora agreed. "You don't have to make any decisions immediately."

"It really helps to be making friends here" I said impulsively. "You have all been so nice and welcoming. It means a lot".

"We like you!" Sorla exclaimed. "We are delighted to know you."

Fergal's father emerged through the back door. He had been up since early mending a fence at the back of their garden.

"Is there a cup of tea left for me?" he asked, as he removed his jacket and hung it on a hook inside the back door.

Fergal stood up. "I'm going to get shaved and dressed and then we can take off whenever you are ready" he said to me.

I nodded assent and started to get up from the table too.

"I'll be a while so take your time" he called out as he made his way upstairs.

I started to gather up dishes to wash up.

"Just bring them over here Una" Nora said. She was already at the sink.

Then in a lower voice she said "I'm so glad he met you. He's been through a rough time".

Sorla and her father were sitting at the table talking and drinking tea, not paying attention to us.

I wasn't sure how to respond to Nora. Did she think Fergal and I were dating?

She continued "That one he was engaged to, I never liked her. I'm glad it is over, but he took it hard."

"I don't know anything about that" I said tentatively, "and you know we just met".

"I know that, but you are nice, and genuine. And he hasn't had a girlfriend since they broke up. So, I am glad he is getting to know you."

"He has been so nice to me" I said. "I'm sure you know he met me at the airport, helped me get a car, drove me to my house that first day. It was way more than I expected anyone to do".

Nora had taken the dirty dishes from me and was busy washing.

"Well, that's Fergal. He has a good heart", she said. "Well, off with you, I can do the rest".

I made my way thoughtfully back to the little guestroom.

TWENTY-NINE

I had decided that I wanted to tell Fergal about my connection with the Donaghys. I hadn't told the entire story to anyone, and I needed to get someone else's opinion. Maybe there was something I was overlooking. Maybe I was jumping to conclusions and I really had no connection to the Donaghys of Krumgedden. Fergal was a lawyer, or soon would be, and I felt I could trust his judgment.

In the car I said, "It was really nice of you to invite me, and I really like your family and your friends."

"Good" he said. "It must be hard not knowing anybody. I can't imagine it myself".

"There is something I want to tell you", I began.

There must have been something in my tone that alerted him because he glanced sideways at me for a second before turning back to look at the road.

"I might be related to the Donaghy's – to Seán Donaghy" I continued. "In fact, I think I am, but it is all so astonishing that I am hoping you can listen objectively and tell me if I am missing something or imagining things".

"Okay. You have my attention now," he said.

I began my story. I began at the beginning, with being raised by Nana, having lost my parents at age 4 and never being able to learn what had happened to them. I talked about my childhood search for my father's family in more detail than I had intended and found myself getting emotional.

"I really wanted to ask your opinion about what I

discovered in the last few days" I said. "I know I am digressing".

"Oh no!" Fergal said. "It is interesting, if sad. I want to hear more, but we are almost at your house. We could go inside if you like, and you could tell me the rest. I don't have to leave for Cork just yet."

"Of course!" I answered. "I can make you coffee in my new coffee-maker."

We did just that. I found some scones and jam. When we were sitting at the kitchen table drinking our coffee, I continued.

I told him about the photo of the elder Frank Donaghy and what Seán Clohessy had said, and about the internet searches revealing the Donaghys living in Saranac Lake, and finally about what Seán Donaghy had told me last night.

He listened quietly and at one point put his hand over mine as it lay on the table between us.

As I presented all the evidence – because that is what I felt I was doing – my uncertainty diminished. I needed to tell the whole story like this to became convinced I was right. Still, I was relieved to hear him say,

"There is strong evidence that this Frank Dinsmore is your father. He is an artist. The man who married Annie in Saranac was an artist. So many pieces fall into place."

He stopped to think for a moment and then said "Tadhg would have been very young when Frank was born – he would have been a teenage father. Is it possible that Frank senior was the father?"

I nodded agreement. "I thought of that too".

"What do you want to do now?" Fergal asked.

"I don't know" I admitted. "I feel so rejected. This man – my father – didn't want to know his family. He abandoned me. What is the point in reaching out to him? He didn't want to know me."

I was on the verge of tears. "And I am angry with Nana that she never told me about him. I feel betrayed by everyone."

"I wonder what his story is" Fergal said.

He was still holding my hand under his on the table, but he was gazing into space, thinking.

"Well, this doesn't mean that the Donaghys in Krumgedden rejected you. They didn't have a chance to meet you, and that would be true for Tadhg too. So, whatever you decide to do about your father, you could still reach out to Seán and Tadhg. And there is value in confirming it – having them confirm it".

"Yes", I agreed. "I might not have found my father, but I could gain a grandfather and cousins."

He was smiling at me now.   "I am glad you told me this."

"I feel so much better, now that I did" I responded.

"I need to go soon but get in touch if you discover anything else or if you need anything."

"I will. Thank you."

"Maybe we can do something next weekend?" He sounded tentative, shy almost.

"I'd like that", I said – an understatement.

I couldn't wait to see him again.

THIRTY

After Fergal left, I found myself looking for whatever I could find about Frank Dinsmore. I knew I was going to do that, despite my protests of anger at being abandoned. I couldn't help myself. I wanted to know everything I could.

There was a photo of the artist, dark-haired, bearded, unsmiling, at an art opening in Manhattan earlier in the year. He was wearing a black sweater and jeans. I stared at the face, searched for any similarity to mine, but couldn't see anything.

The beard didn't help. He looked young – too young to be my father. He had to be in his early fifties in the photo, but he looked like someone in his late thirties.

There was something in the way he was standing that reminded me of the older Frank Donaghy in that old photo, a resemblance I couldn't quite pinpoint.

The Stevens Gallery in Soho had exhibited some of Frank Dinsmore's paintings, along with two other artists, all described as *"Artists depicting New York Post Nine Eleven Angst"*. One painting reproduced in the article appeared to be mostly grey, with ghostly silhouettes of tall buildings.

There were brief biographies of the three artists. Frank had been born in 1966 in upstate New York – the right year and place, I thought grimly.

He had lived in New York since 2003. He had studied at Cooper Union and the Art Students League in New York. There was no mention of what he had done before that.

He currently worked in his studio in Williamsburg, Brooklyn. There was no mention if he lived there or elsewhere. I couldn't find anything about his personal life, marital status, children.

Children! Could I have half-sisters, half-brothers? I hadn't thought of that. I stared again at the face of Frank Dinsmore. The man was a stranger, an enigma.

I wondered if in person as a young man he had looked more like the elder Frank Donaghy in that photo with Josie and Nana, and if Nana had seen the resemblance when she first met him. Had she reacted negatively?   It would have been a double shock – the name and the resemblance if there was one.

I decided, or maybe I knew all along, that even if I didn't want contact with him in the present, I still desperately needed to know what had happened.

Why had he disappeared? Was it as Nana said, that he just couldn't deal with the death of my mother? Or was there more? What had been Nana's role?   Had she made it difficult for him to see me?

Surely Uncle John knew the story. If I told him I had met the Donaghys, would he relent and tell me more? I could try, but I doubted it.

But there was Seán Donaghy. He had openly shared information about Tadhg and Frank.   But he hadn't known then that I might be Frank Dinsmore's daughter. If I told him he might not be so forthcoming.

I sighed. I could wait until Tadhg arrived. If we met, I could then reveal that Annie had been my mother and Frank had been my father and then let him discover the connection.   If he was curious – open to knowing me – he could take the next steps. I didn't want to face more rejection.

My lifelong experience of coming up against resistance to

my questions and information withheld was making me reluctant to pursue this   But I wanted to know so badly.

Yes, I will wait and see first if Tadhg is someone I want to know, want to let into my life, before I tell him. Why open myself up to more rejection?

Having made my decision, I made myself focus on other things   The weather had turned cooler and rainy which encouraged me to stay indoors and work. I threw myself into work on my illustrations for the book project, worked feverishly for hours on end and was able to send copies to Silas ahead of schedule.

THIRTY-ONE

Fergal called and asked if I would like to come into Cork on Saturday. We could spend the day and he could show me around.

I agreed, got directions, and assured him I was okay about driving myself.

I left early on Saturday morning, remembering the advice of the nice girl who worked in the shop next to the supermarket – Dymphna. She had said to drive in early and park in a parking lot, the one she used.

The road was not very busy at 8 am and I found the parking lot without a problem. It was only 8:45. It was way too early to meet Fergal. I felt a little foolish but told myself I had done the right thing. If there had been a lot of traffic or if I got lost, I would have been frazzled. Now I knew how to get here it would be easier the next time.

I walked up two blocks in the general direction of Patrick Street, where I would meet Fergal at 11 o'clock. I passed a small restaurant/bakery and went in to get some coffee.

It had started to drizzle. It was a grey damp-looking day, probably not the best day to walk around sightseeing, but maybe Fergal didn't plan on being outdoors. I hadn't asked what we would be doing. It didn't matter. I just wanted to see him. I had worn my brown leather jacket and had nothing to cover my head. My hair would be a mess I thought ruefully.

I was the only customer in the little cafe. The young red-haired waitress looked up from behind the counter, smiled and said hi.

I went to sit down at a small round table by the window.   I could spot delicious-smelling croissants behind the glass case by the counter. I wanted one. When I saw there were trays and a serve-yourself coffee pot I realized I was supposed to help myself and pay at the counter before sitting down.

As I poured coffee and used tongs to select a croissant the red-haired girl said. "It's getting damp out there" as she gazed out the window.

It was a longing look I thought, as if she wanted to be elsewhere, or wanted the weather to be different for her plans later.

"Yes", I answered. "I am supposed to be sightseeing today. I hope it doesn't rain all day."

The girl looked at me with renewed interest, her attention drawn by my accent.

"It is an unusual time of year for tourists" she said. "How long are you staying in Cork?"

"I will be living in Lockamore for three months. I was in Cork the day I arrived – two weeks ago today but I didn't see much of it" I answered.

She looked ready to ask me more questions but three people came in wanting coffee and pastry to take out, so after paying, I made my way back to my table, carrying my tray.

I stayed for an hour, had a second coffee and another croissant while I read my paperback. It was one I had found among Benjy's books on the history of Cork. I had brought it to show to Fergal.

By ten o'clock there were more customers in the café and more people walking by on the street outside.

It was still drizzling when I left. I found a small store

further down the street that sold umbrellas and bought a cheerful blue and white one, and then found some clothing stores on Patrick Street where I browsed. The sizes were marked differently, and I wasn't too interested in buying clothes anyway. I started to make my way to the housewares section when I noticed the time – ten minutes to eleven. I should leave shortly to meet Fergal at the Bolger Café which was just across the street.

He was waiting outside, standing in the drizzle, hatless and umbrella-less and seeming oblivious to the light rain.

"Fergal, you are getting wet!" I said as I moved to hold my umbrella over him.

"Ah this! It's nothing. Good morning! Did you manage okay driving in? You didn't get lost I hope!"

"I did - get in okay, I mean. I didn't get lost. I got here early and was having a look around," I said, nodding in the direction of the shops across the street.

"Well, shall we go in? I need some coffee. Are you hungry?" he asked as he held the door open for me.

I wasn't that hungry, after my early morning croissants but coffee sounded good, and probably I should eat something too.

The place was bustling and bigger inside than it seemed from outside. We found a table as Fergal said

"It is a pity about the rain, but it might clear up later. There is an art exhibition in the gallery at the University. I thought you might like to have a look. Then if it is not raining too much later, we could take a walk around and see some of the older part of the city - if you are interested, that is."

"Yes, that sounds lovely" I said. He could have suggested anything, and I would have been interested. What was lovely was spending the day with him.

"I found some books on the history of Cork on my uncle Benjy's bookshelf" I said. I didn't have a chance to read them yet, but I brought one with me".

I took it out of my large brown leather bag.

"It is old" he said as he looked at it. He glanced through it. "But it does cover a lot I think."

"There were some other books on local history too, but I hardly know the geography of the area around Lockamore, so I decided to hold off on reading those for a while."

"Don't you have a deadline to work on for your illustrations?" Fergal asked.

"I already sent off the drawings, and I am waiting to hear back. I might have to make changes, or they might send me the next assignment", I answered.

I ended up ordering scrambled eggs and toast. The aroma of the food all around me made me hungry again and we might be skipping lunch or having a very late lunch.

It had stopped raining when we left the restaurant, and a pale sunlight was lighting up the sky.

"I'm amazed at how quickly the weather changes here" I exclaimed. "The rain appears from nowhere and now the sun".

"Well, the rain is not so unpredictable a lot of the time" Fergal said, "But yes, it is nice when a day that starts out rainy turns into a sunny day."

"Do you feel like a walk?" he asked. "It is about 15 minutes to the University."

"Oh, that's nothing" I laughed.

The campus was old and beautiful, and I found it enchanting. There was a wooded walk close by, and we walked silently for a few minutes. I loved the wet leaves of the evergreens glistening in the sunlight and the stark shapes of trees that had lost most of their leaves already. It was late October, and while there was still some colorful foliage, most of the leaves had already fallen.

Fergal suddenly spoke. "Do you have a boyfriend in the States?"

I was startled by the question, maybe because of the setting, or maybe it was the directness of it.

"No." I answered and then hesitated.

There was silence and it seemed I should fill that silence.

"I was seeing someone for about six months. It ended in August. We worked at the same company. That's how I lost my job."

"Oh!" Fergal looked startled. "Was he your boss? Did you get fired?"

"No, nothing like that."

Now I would have to explain.

"When I got back from vacation, I discovered he had started seeing someone else who worked there, so he broke up with me. I quit the next day."

It sounded pathetic, like I'd been so in love and couldn't bear to continue seeing him. It was partly true, but there was more to the story.

"I wasn't doing what I wanted to do at that job. I was getting a paycheck and that was all, so I was going to leave sooner or later. And my Nana had died just a month earlier, so I really needed support not someone else abandoning me."

"You have had a lot to deal with in the past few months" he said. He reached for my hand and held it as we walked.

"And I had no idea about the house in Lockamore until September" I continued, "So with no job and no boyfriend and no family really it seemed like a good time to come here."

"But I am not feeling sorry for myself" I added quickly. "I got my first free-lance illustrating job, and I own my own house."

"Sometimes bad things have to happen to wake us up to what we really want" Fergal said thoughtfully.

I suspected he was talking about himself now. I waited, unsure about how to ask.

"Are you talking from experience?" I finally asked.

"Well, yeah, I suppose so. I'm still trying to figure things out," he said. "I ended a bad relationship last year myself. I really thought we were both committed, and it was the real thing, but it wasn't. It takes a while to get over that sort of thing."

"Yes, it would" I agreed and squeezed his hand in sympathy.

I waited but he said nothing more. We had reached the art gallery.

THIRTY-TWO

The paintings were only mildly interesting to me, not to say they were bad art, just not my style. But I appreciated Fergal's thoughtfulness. Because he saw me as an artist, this is something he thought I would enjoy.

In fact, I was much more intrigued with the old buildings in the university and later when we walked along some small alleys in the older part of the city.

As it got dark and started raining again, we went to meet his friends Declan and Jimmy in a lively pub.

By then I was happy to sit down.   I had been walking most of the day. We gathered around a small corner table, and I thankfully sank onto a banquet while Fergal went to the bar to buy drinks.

Jimmy laughed "I see he has been walking your legs off. He tends to do that."

Finish the sentence, I wanted to say. He tends to do that - with dates, with friends.   Or he walks a lot all the time? What do you mean?

Declan had a girlfriend or a date, Phyllis, who I assumed had been in the bathroom when we arrived and now silently took a seat next to me. She was a bewildered-looking girl with large glasses and shaggy hair.

Declan introduced her. "This is Phyllis"

Fergal reappeared with drinks, including one for Phyllis, so he obviously knew she was here.

I learned that Declan and Fergal shared a flat and Declan was also a law student. Jimmy was a history teacher. They had all known each other since their first year at the University.

I sank back, glad to listen to the conversation about people I didn't know and glad to not be asked again why I was here and not in New York. I knew it was coming unless Fergal had already filled them in on all the details and they didn't need to ask.

It was Phyllis who finally turned to me and asked, "so what kind of art do you like to do?"

I explained about my illustrations for the children's book, and my amusement at the young boy's imagination where he saw his classmates with cabbages for heads.

"There you go Phyllis!" Declan said amused. "What do make of the genetics of that?"

He turned to me "She will probably argue that it is possible. Phyllis loves to argue about genetics."

Phyllis with a mock patronizing air said "Una, Declan doesn't respect scientific discoveries, and he knows nothing about genetics."

"Is that what you do?" I asked.

"I'm a biologist and I am working now in research on genetics" Phyllis explained, "and it is fascinating., and useful also to lawyers, when they want evidence of paternity as Declan well knows."

"Like when you take a DNA test?" I asked doubtfully.

"Yes, that, and blood tests. There are a variety of ways."

Phyllis was about to say more but Declan interrupted.

"So, we heard that you are the last remaining person in your family and inherited a house you never knew existed" he said curiously.

"I knew the house existed, that it was where my grandmother grew up and I knew her brother Benjy lived there, but I didn't know I had inherited it until a few weeks ago." I explained.

"But I have never been in Ireland before, didn't know Benjy had no children", I continued.

"So, what are you going to do?" Phyllis asked curiously. "I mean, you have a life in New York. Are you going to be back and forth?"

Before I could answer Jimmy chimed in. "A lot of people do that. It could be for holidays, your summer home. You could rent it out when you're not here."

"Uncle Benjy was opposed to absentee landlords" I said, "so I wouldn't be renting."

Fergal who had been silent until now said "She's only known about this a little over a month, and she has been in Ireland two weeks, so lads give her a break. She needs time to think."

They all laughed. "Well, we're not demanding answers" Phyllis said. "I am wondering what I would do in such a situation, and I honestly don't know."

That led to speculations of what they would do if someone left them a house on a Greek Island.

Phyllis would continue to work at her job in Cork, because she loved it, but would make frequent trips to the Greek island. Jimmy might move there entirely because of the weather and being sick of the rain in Ireland. Fergal and Declan demanded to know what he would do for money.

Finally, it was time to leave. Jimmy had a late date, and Declan and Phyllis announced they would be off.

I had had two beers but assumed I would be okay to drive, though I wasn't looking forward to driving in the dark and the rain.

Fergal, however, was startled when I said, "I don't know how to get to my car from here."

"You're not driving back to Lockamore tonight?" He looked worried.

When I didn't answer he said, "You can stay at my place of course."

Then holding his hands up as if to defend himself against accusations he said. "I have a couch you can sleep on, no funny business I promise. Declan will stay with Phyllis tonight. Besides, you have been drinking. You don't want the garda pulling you over and giving you a breathalyzer."

"But I only had two drinks" I protested.

"They are very strict here" he said, "Even one drink could put you over the limit and you could end up with paying a fine and having that on your record."

"Is that your lawyerly opinion?" I asked laughing. It was sounding more appealing to sleep over.

He answered soberly. "It is, yeah."

I'll stay of course, thanks" I said.

He put his arm around my shoulder as we walked back in the rain as I held the umbrella over both of us. It was a short walk.

The apartment was on the second floor of a four-floor

building that might have been a large one-family house in the past but was now divided into apartments. It had two bedrooms, a living-room, kitchen, and bathroom, all reasonably tidy.

Fergal asked me if I wanted a cup of tea. Surprisingly I did. I wouldn't normally drink tea late at night, but maybe the rain, and being in Ireland made it appealing.

"There might be some biscuits unless Declan devoured them all" Fergal said rummaging.

He produced a package of digestive biscuits and placed them triumphantly on the table.

We drank our tea companionably. We were sitting on the couch where presumably I would sleep. It was comfortable enough, at least to sit on. I wondered vaguely if he would make any attempt at anything physical, and I wondered how I would respond. I was really attracted to him, but we had both been hurt. What he had said earlier in the day about his difficult relationship led me to think he wanted to take his time, so whatever he might do, it might be smarter for me to slow things down.

My imaginings were interrupted when he suddenly kissed me. I was still chewing a piece of biscuit, which I swallowed hurriedly. If he noticed, it didn't stop him. It ended up being a long kiss and very delicious.

We ended up wrapped around each other and half lying on the couch, our feet still on the floor.

He pulled away eventually, stood up with an air of finality and said,

"You could have my bed if you like, and I'll take the couch."

"No, no" I insisted. "Just give me a pillow and a blanket and I'll be just fine here."

I felt a little disconcerted at the suddenness of his

withdrawal. We had been connecting I thought.

He had already put some folded sheets and a pillow on the coffee table.   I started to arrange them on the couch.

After more cuddling he finally departed towards his bedroom. I felt disappointed as I lay there on the surprisingly comfortable couch, hoping he would come back. He didn't, and eventually I slept.

THIRTY-THREE

When I woke up, it was very quiet. A grey light seeped in through the window. I had slept fine, but I was uneasy. I didn't know what I felt, what I had wanted to happen really.

I lay there thinking.   He was attracted to me, I could feel that, but I could feel the reserve too. Something was holding him back, probably having to do with his past relationship.   There was a need to move slowly. He wanted to move slowly.

His invitation was for Saturday. He didn't feel it was safe for me to drive home last night. That's the reason I was here. He had made it clear when he invited me that was the reason. Why did I feel disappointed and rejected?   It was now Sunday. I should get up and leave early.

It was just after 8 am. I slipped on my clothes quickly and went to the bathroom to splash water on my face, smooth down my hair.

I folded up the blanket and sheets and placed them neatly on top of the pillow.

Now what! Should I just leave without saying goodbye? Try to make some coffee? Wait until he woke up and force him into inviting me to have breakfast with him?

I was still sleepy. I wandered over to the kitchen cabinets. I could make some instant coffee.

No, just leave!

In my bag I found a scrap of paper I had been using as a bookmark in Benjy's history of Cork book, tore it in half and wrote a note.

Thanks for a great day. It was fun. Una.

I placed it on top of the folded-up blanket on the coffee table and silently slipped out of the flat.

Out on the street, empty of people at this hour, I had mixed feelings. I didn't want to leave, yet I was relieved that I had. I understood that we had just started seeing each other yet I felt rejected. Maybe I should have just gone home last night and staying over had been awkward and clumsy. Maybe I should have left the pub early. I was dissatisfied, second guessing myself.

I stopped in confusion at the end of the street, realizing I didn't know how to get back to where I had left the car. I pulled out my phone a punched in my location. About a 20-minute walk it looked like.

I proceeded down two long silent streets and finally turned onto Patrick Street which was a bit more active. There was a place that sold coffee and donuts and I went in thankfully.

The coffee wasn't great, but it woke me up. After the second cup and a large donut I felt more cheerful. Maybe it was the sugar rush. My confident feeling from yesterday started to return. I had had a great long day with a really great guy, who wanted to take it slowly. We would see each other again. I just felt awkward this morning. So, I told myself.

My phone pinged. It was probably Fergal now. It wasn't. It was Deirdre, Seán Clohessy's daughter.

"Ah Una! I hope I'm not ringing too early."

"No, not at all" I said. The large clock on the wall over the counter said 5 past 9.

"I met Julia Flynn yesterday at the supermarket and I told her about you. She would love to see you and wanted me to pass on her phone number."

It took me a moment to remember that Julia Flynn had been one of the girls in the old photo of Nana and Josie. Julia had been one of the girls in pigtails.

"She lives with her daughter on Rossa Avenue" Deirdre was continuing. "It's one of those streets on the other side of the village near the supermarket."

I thanked Deirdre and agreed that I would drop by for a cup of coffee soon and hung up.

The drive back to Lockamore felt easy and familiar. Maybe because traffic was light, maybe because I was getting used to driving. And when I pulled into my driveway, I felt a rush of joy. Yes, my driveway, my house. I looked critically at the front door with its brown peeling paint and thought again of how I needed to paint it a different color - red. Yes, red! That wouldn't be a big job. I would buy paint this week and do it.

Fergal had called while I was driving and left a message, "Sorry I was still asleep. I could have made you breakfast."

He didn't ask for a call back, so I didn't. Instead, I called Julia and was invited to come and visit that afternoon.

THIRTY-FOUR

The woman who answered the phone identified herself as Maura, Julia's daughter.

"Oh yes, Una, isn't it? Deirdre Clohessy was telling us about you. Are you settling in all right?"

I answered with "Yes, everyone is so welcoming".

Maura continued with "My Mam would love to see you. She has been talking about Katey since we met Deirdre. Would you like to come for a visit?"

I said, "I would love to whenever it is convenient."

"The afternoons are easier as it will be quiet here and ye could have a nice chat".

We settled on that afternoon at about 3.

I was curious about Julia about what she could tell me about Nana as a girl, in those first 17 years of her life. She must be the same age as Nana would have been, 91. It would be bittersweet to see her.

I consulted google maps on my phone and saw that Rossa Avenue was on the other side of the village in a small housing estate that stretched at right angles from the road I had driven to the supermarket.

I made a quick stop at the bakery in the shopping mall and picked up some cake on my way and arrived outside number 25 Rossa Avenue at 3.05.

The bright-faced, white-haired woman who answered the door with a welcoming smile reminded me so much of Nana that I did a double-take and my heart turned over.

It wasn't that she looked like Nana exactly. It was just something in her demeanor, or her voice when she said "Una, I am so delighted to meet you". It was so welcoming and familiar somehow.

She led the way into a small front parlor. She moved easily though slowly.

Belatedly, before we sat down, she grasped my hand and shook hands.

She studied my face. "I can see a bit of a resemblance all right" she said. Her eyes were bright and alert.

Maura appeared in the doorway. "Hello Una. Pleased to meet you.

She was a large middle-aged woman. "Sit down there and have a nice chat. I'll make a cup of tea for ye."

That reminded me of the cake. I offered her the bag.

"Oh, you shouldn't have bothered, but it's perfect. Thanks very much".

Maura bustled off.

Julia was already settled in a large blue armchair. The room was warm with a fire crackling cozily. I sat on the matching blue armchair.

I remembered the photo I had found at the house, the one of the four girls. One of them was Julia, Seán had said. I took it out of my bag now and held it out to Julia saying

"I found this at the house with Benjy's things. Seán Clohessy said you were one of the girls".

Julia held out her hand and then studied the photo. I was surprised she wasn't wearing glasses, and it seemed could see perfectly without them.

She laughed and said "The four of us! We were inseparable. I might have seen this a long time ago – oh before they went away. I have some photos too. I'll see if Maura can get them down for me".

She studied the photo, now looking sad.

"And Katey never came back. I thought she might, though her heart was broken when she left. Still, she met someone and got married, so her heart healed".

"Someone broke her heart?" I asked. "A boyfriend?"

"Oh, a fellah she was crazy about. She would have stayed if he had married her. But something happened. She did something."

"Who was he?" I was wildly curious now.

"He was a fellah who was staying with them, helping out on the farm. They had a small farm at the time. He was from close enough, from Krumgedden.   But the poor fellah had no money. There were no jobs to be had back then. Everyone was in the same boat. Not like now. Now you can't get people to work some jobs. Think its beneath them".

Maura came in then with a tray containing a teapot, cups, saucers, a plate of scones, and another plate of sweet biscuits, and there was much activity around setting out the cups, saucers, and plates on the coffee table.

I desperately wanted to hear more about Nana's heartbreak long ago, but Maura took a seat, poured the tea and soon we were talking about life in the U.S. compared to life here and I was answering questions about people I had met and hearing suggestions about who I should meet.

Julia had been studying my face while she sipped her tea. "His name was Frank - Frank Donaghy," she announced.

"Who Mam?" Maura asked, puzzled.

"Oh, the fellow Katey was crazy about before she went to America" Julia said.

She must have seen my eyes widen, heard my sharp intake of breath.

"Maura, you have things to do don't you. I can talk to Una here."

It was a not-so-subtle hint for Maura to leave us alone and for that I was grateful, though I wondered if Julia was confusing Josie with Katey. Josie was the one with the crush on Frank Donaghy - wasn't she?

Maura took the hint seemingly not offended and departed to the kitchen as Julia said, "We used to write letters to each other, Katey and me, when she went over first. She even asked if I ever heard anything about Frank."

"Wasn't it Josie who had the crush on Frank?" I asked.

"Oh, poor Josie, she was always a bit different" Julia answered. "She did, but he had no eyes for her, he only had eyes for Katey and she was serious about him too."

"Do you mean Katey was serious about Frank?" I asked in amazement.

"Oh yes" Julia nodded with conviction. "And we thought he was serious about her too. Oh, the conversations we had, Katey and me, as we imagined the wedding and where they would live. Then the scenes and the heartbreak when he decided to go back to the girlfriend in Krumgedden. Katey had a temper all right. She was enraged. She wanted her revenge and she got it all right."

"Revenge? What did she do?"

I was holding my breath not sure I wanted to hear more, not liking my suspicions.

"It was wrong, what she did, but I never said anything at the time, maybe I should have, but the truth is I felt bad for her at the time and I was mad with him too."

Julia's eyes were bright and clear. She was alert and focused. This was not a senile old lady. She wasn't confusing Nana with Josie. She looked at me directly and said,

"Katey convinced Josie that Frank had tried to molest her, and then she convinced the whole family. Josie was very young, only fifteen, and very childish. The mother and father were shocked. Frank lost his job and had to go back to Krumgedden in disgrace. Shortly after he went to England."

"But Frank never did molest Josie? Is that what you are saying?" I asked.   I needed her to say it.

"No. Josie got her dress caught on barbed wire in the field near where Frank was working and Katey found her crying. She kept asking Josie if she had been near Frank, and it turned out Josie had talked to Frank earlier. Katey kept saying Frank could have been responsible for this., until Josie agreed. Katey told me later what she had done "

"She told you?" I asked.

"Yes, she was telling me how she got a great idea to get back at Frank. It would be punishment for jilting her is what she said."

"My Nana did this!" I mumbled in shock.

"We were all very young" Julia said. "Katey fell hard, and she wasn't used to rejection. She was beautiful you know, there were a lot interested in her. Her pride was hurt."

Julia sighed. "I knew that at the time, and we were close friends. But still, it is no excuse. She damaged a lot of people - Josie as well as Frank. Josie was even more strange after that. She wasn't supposed to go away to America at all, but then she went off with Katey. I used to think it was Katey's way of doing penance, or her way of trying to help Josie. I think she knew she had damaged her. Josie believed the lie. It became real for her. I think Katey had not intended that, but I suppose she didn't think enough of the consequences. I am not sure she ever saw that she had damaged Frank, or if she did, she thought he deserved it."

"Frank went to America too" I said.

"He did. And he married that girl from Krumgedden and took her with him," Julia said.

My shock must have shown on my face, because Julia said, "I have upset you now!"

"No!" I protested. "Well yes, it is upsetting but it is very helpful to know all this, tremendously helpful. I have so many questions about my own parents as well as about Nana.

Julia was puzzled. "Well, Katey never came back, and I never met her children so I can't help you there."

"My father's name was Frank Donaghy" I said in a rush. I didn't know I was going to say it.

Julia stared at me uncomprehendingly.

"Not him, of course, not the Frank you knew, but possibly his grandson, or even his son" I explained.

Juliia's eyes were round. "Oh my! What a turn of events! Well, truth is stranger than fiction."

"I only made the connection in the past few days," I sent on. "I never knew any of this growing up. My mother died when I was a child and my father left me with Nana. I knew nothing about him except his name. Nana - Katey - raised me. She would never talk about my mother or father."

I stopped as Julia reached out and grasped my arm. She looked alarmed. Maybe I had made a mistake in telling her this. She was an elderly lady and maybe it was too much for her.

"You are descended from Frank and Katey" she said.

I had not thought of it like that but of course that is what I now believed.

Maura returned and took away the tea things. Julia had grown quiet. It was time to leave. I promised to come back again to visit.

Julia hugged me before I left and said, "You should visit them in Krumgedden".

THIRTY-FIVE

I was sad and angry over the next few days. The anger wasn't because of the actions of a young girl trying to punish the boy who had jilted her. It was an ugly story, and she might not have understood until later how it would affect Josie, but the urge to get back at Frank was understandable. Still, I didn't think I would have done such a thing at seventeen. Then, I didn't have a boyfriend I was crazy about when I was seventeen.

No, it was what Nana might have done years later that troubled me. What she might have done to her own daughter and to me! I was a pawn in a power struggle. I was collateral damage. And so was my father. That is how it looked to me now. Had she deliberately kept us apart as revenge against Frank?

Had Frank senior been alive when my mother met my father? Probably. The marriage had proceeded. She hadn't succeeded in stopping it. Had she tried?

They might have eloped. They didn't have their families at the wedding at that commune-like place according to the newspaper report.

Had my father known about the history between Nana and his father or grandfather? Had my mother known?

I still couldn't be sure if Frank senior was my great-grandfather. I might not be related to him at all. It could all be a wild coincidence. I couldn't be sure? Or could I?

DNA testing! I remembered the conversation with Phyllis when I was in Cork and her enthusiasm about her job. I wish I had asked her more questions about how they did the testing, what they needed, how close the relationship needed to be to be reliable.

She had given me her phone number. I could call. But I already knew I would need a sample of DNA from one of the Donaghys in Krumgedden.   And I would have to explain why I needed it. But that be enough?

Tadhg would be the most reliable one since it was highly unlikely my father would show up here. Tadhg could be my grandfather unless I had wildly miscalculated.   He would have been a fifteen-year-old father, or sixteen at the most. Or he was my uncle.

From day to day, I changed my mind drastically about what to do. One day I was contemplating calling Seán Donaghy to check on when Tadhg would be arriving and the next, I was so angry with Nana, with all of them for rejecting me that I wanted nothing to do with any of them, including the Donaghys.

And here I was in Benjy's house. Benjy, who had not believed Frank did anything wrong, who alone refused to condemn him, who refused to pass on Nana's letter to him, but who still wrote letters to Nana.

By Friday I was still in a state of indecision when Fergal called. Would I like to get together in Krumgedden or even Lockamore at the weekend?

I said yes. Of course, I said yes.

I said I wanted to tell him about my visit with Julia and ask his opinion about something.

"Mysterious enough" he commented. "There is a nice Italian restaurant not far from Lockamore. We could have dinner there on Saturday."

"Sounds good to me", I said.

He would pick me up at 7 o'clock.

It was a brief phone call, but I needed to tell him in person, not only about Julia, but about my indecision about continuing to investigate my connection to the Donaghys.

Then there was the question about how things would develop between the two of us. I didn't want to seem too eager since he needed to move slowly.

However, it wouldn't hurt to be prepared for all possibilities. I made sure the second bedroom was presentable. He might want to stay over, just as I had stayed over at his place. And I could shop for food in case he stayed for breakfast.

It wasn't clear just how close to Lockamore the Italian restaurant was, or if we would go somewhere else later, or if we would come back here. He was picking me up so he would have to drive me home.

Just play it by ear, I told myself.

****

I drove to the supermarket to stock up on supplies. Eggs and brown bread, tea - the type he had at his place. I would buy some nice mugs and plates at the houseware store, since Benjy's dishes were old and chipped.

I was eyeing the wines, still fascinated that I could buy wine here at the supermarket, when I saw Deirdre emerging from the next aisle, walking briskly, and pushing a full cart.

She looked preoccupied but stopped with a smile and greeted me with a friendly "hello" when I called her name.

"Una! I didn't see you there! How are you! Are you getting used to things here?"

"I am. I like this shopping center", I said, looking around. "Thank you again for putting me in touch with Julia. We had a nice visit, and she remembered my Nana really well," I said.

I wasn't sure if Deirdre knew anything about the incident with Frank Donaghy, but I didn't want to discuss it, so I said nothing. I was embarrassed for Nana, ashamed of what she had done if I was honest.

Deirdre simply commented that Julia was "a great woman - so active and alert."

"She is" I said. "She didn't even need glasses to look at the photos I showed her."

"I'd love to chat longer, Una, but I am in a rush. But I'll be in touch again, maybe you can come over for a visit?" and with that Deirdre rushed off.

I stopped into the housewares store to tell Dymphna that I had successfully found my way to Cork, but she was nowhere in sight. A young, bearded guy at the cash register said it was her day off and that she usually worked weekends.

My phone pinged as I walked out of the store, and I was looking at it, head down when someone called

"Una! Is that you?"

The people I had walked by had stopped and were looking at me. One of them was Seán Donaghy.

"Seán!" I laughed. "This seems like the best place to meet everyone. How are you?"

"I'm grand thanks! Well, it has a lot of stuff here, with all the small shops, so occasionally we come in here, from Krumgedden, but today I'm showing around another Yank. This is my cousin Tadhg,"

My eyes widened as I looked at the man, grey-haired, thin, and searched for a resemblance to Frank Donaghy - either one. The grey hair and thin face didn't look like either Frank, but I didn't want to stare at him too openly.

Seán was continuing. "Tadhg, I'd like you to meet another Donaghy. This is Una Donaghy, also from New York. So ye have something in common."

Tadhg had extended his hand and was shaking mine as Seán spoke.

"Una!" he said, with a sudden alertness, eyes looking searchingly at my face. "Where in New York?" he asked.

"I grew up in Albany but have been living in New York City" I answered.

Now was my chance to say - what? Was it wise to blurt out that we might be related?

Seán, however, volunteered. "Una is here because her grand-uncle left his house to her in Lockamore, and she is thinking of moving back."

Tadhg looked interested. "I am here to try to buy a house. I'm going to move here altogether when I retire in a few months."

"I only found out about the house in September." I explained. My Nana left the house to me. She was Benjy's brother."

"Benjy Loughlin", Seán chimed in. "You might not remember them. His sister Katey was Una's grandmother."

"Katey Loughlin was your grandmother?" Tadhg was staring at me intensely. "I knew who Katey Loughlin is. And did you say your last name is Donaghy?

He knows who I am. Oh God, what's going to happen now? Well, here goes.

"Yes, it is. My father's name was Frank Donaghy, but I don't know anything about him. My mother died when I was 4 and I'm not sure what happened to my father."

My voice had faltered because he was staring at me so fixedly.

"You are Frank's daughter! And your mother! Was her name Annie?"

"Yes."

I could say no more. I waited.

Then he said, "Frank is my son."

I said nothing.

He said "Frank's wife Annie died. They had a little girl. Her name was Una. I must be your grandfather."

Now that he was sure I was strangely unsure, strangely reluctant to accept that this was my family. I had an perverse urge to argue that it might not be true.

I said, "I never knew where my father's people came from. No-one told me they were from this area too. I thought it was just a coincidence when I heard the name Donaghy here."

Then I added "Are you sure?"

"What else could it be?" Tadhg said.

Seán had been silent. Now he said "And your father? Are you in touch?"

"No, I don't know where he is or anything about him."

That was not true of course, because thanks to Seán I had figured out he was now calling himself Frank Dinsmore and was a New York artist. And I knew that Tadhg's son was Frank Dinsmore.

"Well, well" Seán was murmuring, obviously at a loss for words.

Tadhg too seemed to be stunned.

I had to say something, or we would continue standing here staring at each other.

"You said you knew Katey Loughlin" I began. "What do you know about her?"

"Oh, I never met her, but my father knew her. My father used to work on the farm of - well it must have been your great-grandfather. He knew Katey and Benjy.   When Frank met Annie, we didn't know at first that Katey was Annie's mother. We only knew because Frank told us that Annie's family was from Lockamore and my parents were curious and so Frank asked Annie what her mother's maiden name was. Frank knew nothing about the past, thought it was something interesting to report back to Katey, that his parents were from the same place. But she took it badly it seems, and Frank didn't understand. He said Katie wanted Annie to stop seeing him."

As he talked, I knew of course Tadhg had to be my grandfather.   I had been protecting myself, not wanting to believe it without proof, but this was what I had suspected all along. Nana had not liked it that my father was related to that other Frank who had rejected her.

Seán had reached his hand out as if to support me.

"You are in shock, love. You are very pale. We should sit down someplace."

"Yes" Tadhg said. "We should sit down and have a cup of tea." He led me into the little café I had found my first morning here. We ordered tea and scones.

THIRTY-SIX

After my encounter with Tadhg and Seán I spent the rest of Friday and most of Saturday trying to acclimatize myself to my new status. It took some getting used to -being part of a big family. I was invited to visit Seán's family on Sunday for dinner. They would all know about me, and I knew nothing about them.

I hadn't learned much about the family while we had tea at the shopping center.   I was incapable of absorbing any information and they seemed to understand that. We stuck to safer topics - Uncle Benjy's house, driving on the other side, my drawing and painting, Tadhg's plans to move to Ireland. I learned his wife had come with him, but she was not my grandmother. Tadhg didn't say more, and I didn't ask. I had enough to deal with already.

I was looking forward to seeing Fergal. Things had changed so much since we had made our plans to have dinner. There was even more to talk about now.

When Fergal arrived, I rushed to open the door in a cloud of newly acquired perfume, something called La Vie en Rose, which I had bought yesterday before meeting Seán and Tadhg, when I was still focused on my upcoming date. I forgot about the perfume afterwards. All I could do was drive myself home in a daze, all other thoughts gone from my head. I found it just before Fergal was to arrive and sprayed it on in a rush.

He kissed me - really kissed me, not just a peck on the cheek- when I opened the door. I responded enthusiastically.

"It's so good to see you", he mumbled, face buried in my hair.

"It's good to see you too" I responded.

"It seems different here" he said, looking around the hall and living room while I put on my coat and grabbed my purse.

"I didn't make any changes here" I said puzzled, and then remembered, "Oh yes, I did move this", pointing to the small hall table which had been right inside the entrance which I had moved back and to the side. I had taken a lamp from the bedroom upstairs and placed it on the table as well as a basket I had bought at Hamptons.

"It looks different?" I asked, pleased.

"Yes, more lived-in and sort of elegant."

I laughed. "I like this place but elegant is not a word I would use to describe it. Cozy, now that is an appealing word."

"Well, it is elegant in a lived-in way not in a hands-off way." Fergal protested.

"Did you see the little room I am using for my work-space"? I asked, leading the way down the hall.

Fergal hadn't, as on that first day when I arrived with him, I thought the door led to a closet and we hadn't opened it. Now he looked around impressed.

"What a perfect room! A secret room!" he exclaimed.

"A secret room is just what I thought when I discovered it first" I said. "And it seems to be part of the original house too."

"Yeah, I wonder what the purpose was" Fergal said.

At my look of surprise, he continued "Was it constructed to hide people or ... Do you know when the house was built?"

"I don't," I confessed, "but there are some books of local history here in the bookcase. I didn't get a chance to read them yet."

"Why?" I continued. "What would they want to hide?"

"People possibly" he answered. "I did hear that during the civil war this house was a gathering place. They could have had meetings in here."

"But people could be seen entering or leaving the house" I said puzzled.

"Look at how close it is to the back door" he said. "Someone could slip out the back and disappear into the fields".

That reminded me of the day I had discovered the graveyard, when I had walked over the fields after seeing Liam and had made my way to the back door of the house sitting in darkness. I shivered as I remembered how dark it was with no house lights to illuminate the darkness.

Fergal was continuing. "This house is older than that though, so going back well over a hundred years before independence."

I stared around the room with a new fascination.

"There is so much to learn" I said. "I can hardly keep up."

We had started making our way out to Fergal's car as I said, "I met my grandfather yesterday."

Fergal stopped. "You sound very certain of that".

"I still like the idea of getting a DNA test, but I'm pretty sure now that Tadhg is my grandfather."

As we drove to the restaurant, I told him about my encounter with Seán and Tadhg at the shopping center.

"And so, I suddenly find myself part of a big family" I said wonderingly. "Somehow, when I wanted to find my father, I had never considered that. Oh, maybe when I was a child, I dreamt of having cousins and grandparents, but in the past few months I didn't think of that." I trailed off.

"I suppose it takes getting used to" Fergal said sympathetically.

The restaurant was quite upscale, with linen tablecloths, lots of silverware and sparkling glasses. The staff was friendly and welcoming and the food excellent. Fergal had tried to make this a special occasion and I gave him and the food my full attention. We shared a bottle of wine and lingered talking after we had finished eating.

"Will you contact your father?" Fergal asked.

"I am not sure" I said slowly. "I will take it day by day, I think. When I see Tadhg tomorrow, I will try to find out if he is in contact with Frank. He might even have told him about me already. Yes, I might just let him make the first move."

"Unless he has cut himself off from the family completely" Fergal said. "But why?" I can understand if he and your grandmother were alienated, but why cut himself off from his own family?"

"I don't understand it" I said sadly. "But I don't know him. It's Nana I don't understand. I thought I knew her so well. She was like a mother to me for as long as I can remember, but now it looks like she stopped my father from seeing me."

"Maybe she blamed him for your mother's death, or for her illness," Fergal suggested.

"Possibly, but I am afraid that she might have held a grudge from the past too, but now I will never know", I sighed

"Did you realize you have another grandmother who may still be alive?" he asked.

"Yes! I mean no I haven't really thought about it" I said wonderingly, remembering what the records had revealed.

"Tadhg was about sixteen when my father was born, and he grew up with Tadhg and the elder Frank and Eileen. That's why I couldn't find a record of him in Albany."

"So, Tadhg might never have married your grandmother" Fergal said.

"She would be about the same age as Tadhg, about sixty," I said. "But my father grew up with Tadhg and his grandparents, not with her. I wonder why."

"You could have even more cousins if she had more children" Fergal said.

"I'm scared", I said. I suddenly started to feel overwhelmed. "I mean, it is irrational, because this is what I wanted for so long. But I got used to my solitary state and now it is almost too much. What if I don't like them? What if I regret letting them know who I am? What if they don't like me?"

"You could always go back to New York and disappear and never be heard from again" Fergal said with a laugh, but he was watching me, a question in his eyes.

"I hope you don't, but you could." He was waiting for an answer.

"I am not going to disappear" I said, holding his gaze "especially from you. I am happy to have met you."

"Me too" he answered softly, reaching for my hand across the table.

"How about if we get out of here?"

THIRTY-SEVEN

There was no mention about anyone sleeping on a couch that night. In fact, there was no discussion at all. He drove us back to my house and led me upstairs and we fell into bed.

I wasn't about to ask what had changed his mind. Whatever developed between us in the future, right now I needed this - to be close, to be loved, to be accepted.

He was wrapped around me on the bed both of us still fully clothed.   He pulled back and cupped my face in both of his hands and stared intently into my eyes.

"I feel so connected, like we really know each other, but it's been such a short time," he said. "I don't know. Am I moving too fast?"

"No", I said. "I feel that connection too. I want to know you. I mean, I want you in my life in whatever way that can happen."

That was the end of talking for awhile as we started to get undressed. My red scarf was still around my neck. That and my shoes were the first to go.

****

I woke up to the aroma of coffee brewing. He was already up and downstairs. I lay there contentedly, happy that he felt comfortable enough to make coffee, happy that we were now together.'

He appeared in the doorway, hair on end, bare-chested,

wearing only pants and carrying two of the large yellow mugs I had bought, a big smile on his face.

"You are awake! I was trying to be quiet, but I brought you up some coffee just in case."

He placed the mugs on the side table and kissed me. "You are so beautiful!"

"You are kidding" I said, surprised but pleased. "My hair must be sticking out at all angles and I'm sure I have morning breath."

I knew the thing to do was accept the compliment gracefully and not draw attention to my shortcomings, but I wasn't good at that.

"I like the tousled look, what can I say", he grinned as he ran his hands through my hair and pushed some of it into my face.

"Ok, I'll leave you in peace to have your coffee" he said relenting as he grabbed one of the mugs and propped himself next to me on the bed.

I was oddly shy, wondering if we were now to discuss our "relationship", and was relieved when he asked what time I had to be at the Donaghy's.

"They said one pm" I answered. "It's an early Sunday dinner. I don't know who exactly will be there, but I'm a bit anxious about being the center of attention."

"Well, they want to meet you. That's a good thing, isn't it? And I know my parents like Seán and Maura his wife. They have three children, Liam is away in Dublin, so he mightn't be home, Nuala is in Limerick, and there is Sheila who is about sixteen or seventeen. She might be there."

"So, it's not a huge family, but there might be cousins," I said.

"There might be," Fergal agreed, "but they are disposed to like you. Just be yourself."

"What will you do?" I asked. "You could stay here of course if you like."

"I'll go and visit my parents for a few hours and then go back to Cork - unless" he hesitated "if you need me, I'll just be down the road at my parents. You can always text me."

"I don't know how long I'm expected to stay, but I'm sure it will be fine. I'll definitely text you later and let you know how it went," I promised.

We eventually made our way to the kitchen and made some eggs and toast.

"Is it okay to tell my parents that you are related to the Donaghys?" he asked before leaving. "I know they'll be interested and probably delighted."

"Of course!" I answered. "I think everyone is bound to know soon anyway. There is no need to keep it a secret."

He hugged me tight before leaving and whispered, "I can't wait to see you again."

The warm glow stayed with me as I got ready to meet my family. I didn't want to say goodbye to Fergal, but I needed to prepare myself for the visit.   First impressions were important.

I was almost ready to leave when I realized I should have picked up something - a cake, or dessert of some sort to take with me. Well, too late now!

Or maybe it wasn't. I could get some chocolates or even a cake at the shopping center before driving to Krumgedden. I just needed to leave now and stop dawdling.

It only took a few minutes to get a cake and some chocolates. In fact, I thought I would arrive too early, but I ended up being a little late, because when I got to Krumgedden, I took the wrong turn and drove quite a distance along the wrong road before I realized my mistake. I was a little frazzled when I finally arrived and wasn't all that sure it was the right house.

Seán, however, must have been looking out for me because he flung open the door and waved while I was still in the car. He was beaming which put me at ease right away. I remembered how kind and friendly he had been and knew this would be all right.

"You found us!" he shouted. "Come in!"

Tadhg appeared at the door as I walked up. Together they led me inside.

THIRTY-EIGHT

The living room was cozy, with a fire going and there was a delicious smell of cooking food wafting from somewhere nearby. A pair of curious eyes greeted me. One pair belonged to a petite white-haired woman and the other to a tall girl in her teens with long brown hair.

The girl said "I remember you! You were with Fergal Sullivan last week at Orla's party."

The white-haired woman grasped my hands and said "Una, I am so pleased to meet you! I am Joanne, Tadhg's wife."

The girl was Sheila, Seán's youngest child. His other two children were away in Dublin and somewhere else and couldn't be here.

Maura, Seán's wife, appeared then, wearing an apron, and also greeted me with "Yes, I remember seeing you with Fergal and thinking what a pretty girlfriend he found for himself. Little did I know! Welcome my dear! It's lovely to meet you.!"

The conversation was easy after that as I explained about Matt O'Sullivan being the lawyer who had dealt with Benjy's will and how he had sent Fergal to meet me at the airport when I arrived.

"So, you had no idea that you were related to us?" Sheila asked.

"No idea," I said. "I never knew my father - at least since I was four years old, when my mother died but I don't remember him and never learned anything about him after that."

I looked at Tadhg. "My grandmother and uncle never told me anything, but I was curious, and in my teens, I tried to find a record of my father. I always thought my parents met at school, at St. Agnes in Albany. That was where my uncle went to school and I guessed it was where my mother went, but I couldn't find any Frank Donaghy."

"Your father didn't go to St. Agnes" Tadhg responded, "but I did."

We were now gathered around the table, and were being served roast potatoes, brussels sprouts, and roast beef, all looking and smelling delicious. Tadhg was sitting next to me.

Tadhg was continuing. "Joanne is not Frank's mother. I think you gathered that already. I was very young when I discovered that my girlfriend at St. Agnes was pregnant. It was a big scandal in those days. We did the right thing and got married. But we were sixteen. We were too young."

Tadhg stopped eating and he gazed at the opposite wall, remembering.

"For a year we lived with her parents, and I continued at school. She dropped out unfortunately, or really was forced to drop out. Her parents thought it would be too much of a scandal to have her appear at school when she was pregnant. She was an intelligent girl from a very strict family and resented not being able to graduate. She had dreams of going to college. She became very angry, with her parents, with me - and one day she just left."

Sheila, sitting on the other side of Tadhg was listening entranced.

"Do you mean she ran away?" she asked.

"I suppose so, but she told me she was leaving. She wanted me to take the baby, so I did and moved back to my parents who had moved out of Albany by then to the country. I finished High School in Saranac and went to college after that, and

Connie and I eventually got a divorce. My parents were happy to raise Frank. I was there a lot, but I was a young man. By the time I married Joanne Frank was 12 and he wanted to continue living with my mother and father, so he did."

Tadhg looked at me sadly. "I wanted to be a good father. I hope I did the right thing for him. There was a tight bond between him and my parents."

"But he disappeared just like his mother did" I said before I could stop myself. "Did she ever come back, or make contact? Did she try to see him?"

"Not when he was a child. It was her parents she really resented because they forced the marriage and forced her to drop out of school. And she was very young."

I was aware that the rest of the table had grown silent and that everyone was now listening to Tadhg. I imagined that this story of his first marriage was not one they were used to hearing, or not in such detail. He had been so engrossed in his memories that he hadn't been aware of this until now.

I sensed that he didn't want to continue. I understood his reluctance, but I desperately wanted this to continue as a private discussion. I was grateful that he was so willing to share these details with me. I wanted to know more about this grandmother - my other grandmother - and her family.

"Times have changed, especially here" Maura said. "Now the trend is to live together, have a child and then get married, no apologies to anyone. Mind you, it is a bit too lax in my opinion, but it is an improvement over the past when girls were shamed into marriage when they weren't ready."

Sheila said "Dad said you were living in New York before coming here. That must be quite a change."

That led to me talking about New York and about my former job, and my apartment. Tadhg was surprised and interested when I mentioned that I was working here on the illustrations for the children's book.

"Oh, you are an artist too!" he said, looking at me in wonder. "You know that your father is."

"Yes, he is an artist and lives in New York" I finished. "We could have been living blocks from each other."

Again, I could see Tadhg really wanted to talk about Frank but didn't want an audience.   Maura seemed to pick up on this. When dinner was finished Maura said, "why don't the two of you go in here and have a bit of a private chat before the cousins arrive," as she led us to a small sitting room.

Once seated, Tadhg launched in immediately.   "I am in touch with your father, and he was always close to his grandparents. Honestly, I think he felt they were his real parents. But we had a good relationship when he was growing up, there was no animosity."

"Do you know why he left after my mother died?" I asked the question that was after all so central to my life.

"There was always friction between him and Katey. Piecing things together after the fact this is how I understand it. When she heard his name first, she had a strong reaction. Because he knew she was from Ireland he thought she was interested in his Irish background. He said he was called after his grandfather, also named Frank Donaghy from Krumgedden. It seems she clammed up."

"Frank, of course, knew the story of his grandfather and Katey Loughlin, but Katey was now known as Katey McCarthy, or Mrs. McCarthy. Frank didn't make the connection and didn't know where exactly Katey had grown up. It was only later that he learned from Annie that her mother's maiden name was Loughlin from Lockamore. "

"My father was surprised, but he loved Frank and would have been reconciled to meeting Katey. He told us that Josie and Katey had lied and that he had never done anything to Josie. We believed him. Annie, it seems, thought it was all ridiculous and believed that Josie was very unstable and could have imagined the whole thing. It was Katey who seemed to still hold on to the grudge and was opposed to Frank and Annie being married."

I realized that Tadhg didn't know that Nana had been in love with his father. Maybe the elder Frank had never shared that.

Tadhg continued, "But they joined an artist's colony and got married there and we only found out later. It was a disappointment to my mother especially, but I could understand the difficulties of young people in love who see parents as the obstacle after what I had been through myself."

"We did see you when you were a baby". He smiled at my surprise.

"Yes, they came to visit us in Saranac and brought you to meet us, but it was only that once. Your mother was charming, beautiful, and we could see she really loved the two of you. We thought it would be the beginning of many visits, but that was not to be."

He sighed and reached out to grasp my hand. "But here you are. Life is strange that you should come back to us through Katey's actions."

"How did I end up with Nana - with Katey?" I asked.

Tadhg looked at me sadly. "Frank was truly devastated at the loss of Annie. Questions were raised about the group - commune, I suppose where they lived and if the death was suspicious. Frank was in the middle of an investigation. Katey accused Frank of being the cause of Annie's death and said she would sue for custody of the baby - you. Frank was so heartbroken and already blaming himself for Annie's death. He was the one who had discovered this group, who wanted to live there, so he felt responsible in that way. I think it was his guilt and his feeling of worthlessness, more than the threat of the lawsuit that did it, so he let her take you, but I believe he never meant for it to be permanent."

"But then he never came back for me" I said sadly.

Tadhg looked sharply at me, a question in his eyes.

"Is that what you think? But he did. He tried many times. She put him off, saying you needed to stay with her longer, then you were in school, and your life would be disrupted. Later she again threatened a lawsuit. Frank had already moved to New York by then. He was young and poor, a single father. I think he just gave up after that."

"But he never even called me, wrote to me" I protested.

"That was the agreement. He was to have no contact with you," Tadhg said.

But I wasn't willing to accept that so easily. "He was my father. He had rights. Why didn't he sue her for custody?"

"He didn't think he could win I suppose" Tadhg sighed. "But you would have to ask him."

There was a silence as I tried to absorb this.

As if he anticipated my next question, Tadhg said "He would really like to see you."

"He knows?" I stuttered. "He knows about me?"

"I let him know that day, the day we met in the shopping center. I phoned him later and told him."

"He must have been surprised" I said tentatively. I really wanted to ask *Is he glad? Does he want to see me?*

"He was amazed, Tadhg agreed, "But he was happy you were going to meet the family. He would like to talk to you but would leave it up to you if you want to be in touch with him."

I must have looked uncertain because again he squeezed my hand and said, "He does want to know you Una, but he is afraid you might be more reluctant."

Why doesn't he come rushing to see his long-lost daughter? Why must I be the one to seek him out - yet again.

I felt mutinous.

THIRTY-NINE

The cousins arrived and that put an end to the conversation between Tadhg and me.

There were many cousins all curious and asking the same questions. I tried but gave up on remembering names and relationships and was grateful when Maura called me into the kitchen for "a quiet cup of tea".

"It must be overwhelming for you" she said sympathetically. "Take a little break here for a while. They'll be leaving soon anyway."

"They are so welcoming, and that is great" I said, "But it is hard to keep all the names straight. I probably won't remember."

"Ah, that's all right. They'll understand" Maura assured me.

We sat in comfortable silence sipping our tea. My mind was in turmoil. I really needed to be alone to sort all this out, but Nora seemed to understand even though she said nothing. I knew I was blaming my father to avoid blaming Nana for pushing him away. I was still holding onto the image of my Nana, the only mother I had known.

Sure enough, eventually there were rumblings of imminent departure from the living room and one friendly cousin stuck her head through the kitchen door to say good-bye.

Maura said, "We should probably go out now to see them off".

Before long the entire group had left, not before many goodbyes and promises to be in touch.

I left then, again with promises to stay in touch, and assuring them that I could easily find my way back to Lockamore on the dark road. I wasn't so sure of that, but I needed to be alone now.

On the way back I wondered if I could cope with all this family or if I was too much of an introvert. I had never thought seen myself as an introvert before, but I did feel overwhelmed. It had been a long day.

****

I got back without incident. It was very dark, almost Halloween, but I must be getting used to being here, or I was just too preoccupied.

I called Fergal as soon as I got into the house. He was already back at his flat.

"It was a long day for you" he said sympathetically.

"They are all really nice, and lots of cousins came to visit, but there were so many. And Tadhg talked about my father and my Nana." I was almost sobbing and tried to remain calm.

"Oh! He did!" Fergal was alert. "Did he mention conflict?"

"She threatened to bring a law-suit if he didn't stay away" I gasped. "Oh, it is a complicated story, about my mother's death and how she blamed my father. It is so devastating that my Nana who I loved so much did this. But I'm mad with him too. Why didn't he fight for me?"

"You need time to sort it out. You don't have to do anything. Just take the time you need," Fergal said.

"You are such a good friend" I said, "I mean as well as you know - but you really are a good friend."

"As well as being a really good lover - Is that what you are telling me?" he said laughing.

I laughed too and it lightened my mood. "Yes, something like that. I appreciate your many qualities."

I was tired then, but it took a while for me to sleep. There were so many questions left unanswered.

FORTY

Winter set in in earnest as soon as November started. It was wet and dark outside. I got more assignments from Silas Van Doren and stayed inside in my little study with the fire on. I immersed myself in my work and tried not to think of my father.

I invited Tadhg and Joanne to visit for dinner one evening and showed them the house. I invited Seán and Maura too, but they declined saying "another time, spend the time with your grandfather."

They admired the house and the acreage. Tadhg wanted a garden and a place to grow vegetables. They had a couple of possibilities in mind, but both were at a distance from Krumgedden and they were trying to make up their minds. They had to be back in New York before Thanksgiving, as Tadhg was still working and had taken some vacation time. They would like to have made an offer on a house before then but it didn't seem likely to happen.

"If there is anything I can do let me know" I said doubtfully.

I had a reservation on a return flight to JFK for January 16th, but I was very unsure about what I should do after that.

"Seán knows everyone around here" Tadhg assured me. "He can handle things for me. But if we make a decision on a place before we leave maybe you can come and take a look and give us your opinion."

Joanne looked with kind but critical eyes around the kitchen and agreed it needed an update. They both loved the study and were admiring of my illustrations which were scattered on the round table.

I discovered that Tadhg and Joanne had three children, Jason who was 30, Sandy 28, and Louise 26 - my aunts and uncle!

"When you are back in New York you will have to come and visit us and meet them," Joanne said enthusiastically.

She turned to Tadhg. "Thanksgiving would be perfect as everyone would be there. Of course, it might be our last Thanksgiving all together". She said this sadly.

"There will be lots of opportunity for visits back and forth, and besides they are all living at a distance from us now," I thought this was a statement Tadhg had made many times already.

"And Frank - my father - does he have any other children?" I asked hesitantly. They had refrained from mentioning my father after that long exchange when I visited Seán's house, and I wasn't sure why.

"No, he has no other children," Tadhg answered. "It's another reason why the two of you shouldn't be apart."

He glanced at Joanne. "Yes, I know I should stay out of it, but they should at least make contact."

It had been two weeks since the dinner at Seán's house and I had felt confused and angry. Tadhg had said he told my father about our meeting. I suppose I was waiting for some gesture from him. Let him make the first move!

"He was very interested you know. He wanted to know all about you. He wants you to call him. He wants to talk to you." Tadhg said. He held his hands up, "but it is up to you. I don't mean to interfere."

"If he is so interested, why doesn't he call me?" I burst out in exasperation. "There is no Nana now to stop him and he still doesn't contact me."

Tadhg looked surprised. "Would you like him to call you? I think he would be glad to. I think he was afraid you wouldn't want to talk to him and was letting you make the first move."

But now I was angry. The pent-up rage and resentment of the past couple of weeks came tumbling out.

"He is the one who stayed away all this time, even after I was grown up and living on my own - in New York for heaven's sake where he lives. He could easily have reached out to me. I don't really believe he wants to know me."

"I don't think he knew you were living in New York" Tadhg said bewildered.

Joanne looked worried. She now said thoughtfully, "There has been so much miscommunication. The only way to sort it out is for the two of you to talk. It would be better in person, but a phone call would be better than nothing."

She turned to Tadhg. "You could ask him to phone Una. Would that be okay Una?"

I nodded numbly already embarrassed at my outburst. They had just been trying to help, had been trying to be sensitive to my wishes. Maybe I had been giving off mixed signals. I was certainly confused enough, and very fearful too. I had to acknowledge that if only to myself. There was that fear of what would happen when - if - we talked.

****

The call came the next day in the evening. My cell phone displayed the name Frank Dinsmore.

I answered hesitantly "hello".

His voice in turn was hesitant, sounding surprisingly young.

"Is this Una?"

"Yes. Hello."

Again, the hesitation. "My father said it was okay to call you. Is it?"

"Yes, of course."

This was awkward. This would have been better in person. Then I realized he was probably as terrified as I was. That gave me courage.

"It was so amazing to discover that Tadhg was my grandfather. And of course, before that it was amazing to have inherited this house in Lockamore, and then to discover I was related to the Donaghy's in Krumgedden." I was babbling, but it seemed to have loosened something in him too.

"I didn't know anything until my father called me. I was led to believe you hated me and wanted nothing to do with me." He broke off in confusion. "I'm not trying to blame anyone."

"They told me nothing about you" I said, "only that you had been devastated after my mother died and left. I knew nothing about Nana's attempts to keep you away, not until I talked to Tadhg. And no, I didn't hate you. I tried to find you, but no-one would help me - when I was younger that is."

"I did think of you and wanted to see you" he said sadly, but as time passed, I became convinced that it was better for you to leave you where you were."

"I was happy with Nana" I admitted. "In fact, it is only now after her death I am discovering this other side of her, and it is hard to deal with."

"You know, it is a long and complicated story and something we should talk about in person, if you would like to that is," he said.

"Yes, I would like that", I said shyly. "I will be back in New York in January. Maybe we can meet then?" I had decided in that moment I would go back as planned. After that I still didn't know what would happen.

After that we talked about other less loaded topics. He was interested in my art; I was interested in his. He talked animatedly about his latest project. I realized we had interests in common. He described his studio. We both became light and giddy - relief on both sides probably now that the first difficult contact had been made. We promised to be in touch again.

After that he called me regularly once a week and we got to know about each other's life. He confessed that he had never been particularly interested in visiting Ireland but that now he would think about it.

He didn't say but I gathered he wasn't particularly close to his stepsiblings. He seemed to not be in contact with relatives in general.

FORTY-ONE

Fergal and I fell into a regular routine. We would spend the weekend together either in Lockamore or in Cork where I would stay at his flat, this time always sleeping in his bed.

I became more friendly with Phyllis, who was fascinated with my story and asked if I wanted DNA testing.

"I don't think it is necessary" I said, "and I don't want to insult anybody by suggesting it. Things are good right now, but we are all still getting to know each other."

"Imagine, that old photo you found of your grandmother and your great-grandfather - maybe they were destined to bring you into the world one way or another."

Phyllis was dedicated to her science, but I noticed a fatalistic streak that emerged at times.

"You are such a romantic!" I laughed. But secretly I was pleased.

I still hadn't quite accepted my Nana as a vengeful person and had to resign myself to the knowledge that there had been a whole side to her that she had hidden from me. I wondered what my mother had thought, and now I was excitedly anticipating the meeting with my father and hearing all about my mother too.

I spent Christmas with Fergal at his family's house in Krumgedden. His mother couldn't hide her delight that we were "going steady" and whispered to me that she hadn't seen him so happy in a long time.

I was still uncertain about what would happen in the future, but I was planning to spend a couple of months in New

York, and to try to line up more freelance art projects. Silas had said the author was pleased with my illustrations for her book, so I would go and see him. I would see if Sandra wanted to continue to sublet. She was willing to share with me while I was there. I thought she would agree as we got along fine, and she would have the apartment to herself again when I returned to Ireland.

But of course, my main goal was to spend time with my father - I still couldn't quite believe it - my father! I had learned more about him in our weekly conversations. There was a reticence which was diminishing as we talked more.

Fergal drove me to the airport on the cold January day I left, and I marveled at how much had happened, and at how close Fergal and I had become since that day I arrived when he picked me up at this same airport.

I promised him I would be back in April. Beyond that I didn't know. I would miss him and wanted him in my life, but it was confusing. I now lived in two different places, and I felt pulled in two different directions. I hated leaving him, but I was excited about returning to New York and seeing my friends. We promised to call or text every day. It was hard saying good-bye, but I promised I would be back before he knew it.

I was tearful on the plane as I watched the little green fields and stone walls below disappear and give way to just sky as the plane climbed higher. This time there were no chatty old Irish ladies, just younger business-like people. I didn't feel like talking to anyone, so that was a good thing.

New York was jarring, frighteningly fast-paced, strange yet familiar all at once. I felt dazed, slow-moving, as I made my way from the airport.

The apartment was neat as a pin. Sandra was still at work but left a little note propped up on the table saying, "Welcome

Home." She had been very willing to share with me for two months and to continue subletting indefinitely after that. I had insisted that I would sleep on the couch.

I felt a pang of sadness as I looked around my apartment, no longer really mine, and felt confused again about my future. It had been such an achievement to find this apartment and to furnish it. As my friends had reminded me, you don't just give up a good apartment with reasonable rent in New York. You hang onto it. But I couldn't be in two places at once.

Sandra arrived and we made dinner and talked for a couple of hours until I was overtaken by jetlag. She considerately removed herself to the bedroom though it was much too early for her to sleep, while I pulled out the couch and was soundly asleep in a matter of minutes.

I woke disoriented. It was dark and around 4 am, but now I was fully awake thanks to jetlag. My body thought it was five hours later. The good thing about sleeping in the living-room was that it was in between the kitchen and the bathroom on one side and the bedroom on the other. I could move around quietly without walking Sandra.

I hadn't unpacked and my suitcase was still standing right inside the door. I could get out a change of clothes, take a shower, make some coffee. I knew from experience, when friends had crashed on my couch that any bathroom noises wouldn't carry into the bedroom, although the smell of coffee might. But it wouldn't wake her would it, the smell? No, I reasoned, she would only smell the coffee when she woke up.

Showered and dressed, I sipped my coffee and sent some texts to friends announcing I was back. They were all still asleep of course, but they would respond later, and we would make plans to get together.

I also sent a text to Frank - my father - that simply said *I am back in New York, would love to meet whenever you want.*

I hesitated about contacting Uncle John and decided that for now I wouldn't tell him I was back. I suppose I needed to have a confrontation with him, but I wasn't ready yet. I had been in touch with him only sporadically since I had met Tadhg. I hadn't told him that I had been in contact with my father.

I didn't know how much Uncle John knew about Nana's history, or what she had told him about my father. At first, I had been almost as angry with him as I had been with Nana, but over the past couple of months I realized that Nana would never have told him about her involvement with the older Frank. But he must have believed that it was best that my father was kept from contacting me.

Sandra emerged sleepily at 6:30 and disappeared into the bathroom. I had made a full pot of coffee and she gratefully helped herself to a mug as she disappeared back to the bedroom to get dressed.

I toasted some muffins and made a mental note to pick up some food later.

"I made some space so that you can hang your clothes" Sandra said as she came back to the kitchen now fully dressed. I saw that her uniform of grey and black with a crisp blouse hadn't changed.

She refilled her coffee mug as she sat at the kitchen table.

"Is this one for me?" she asked, reaching for one of the muffins.

I nodded mouth full. "I was awake so early. I hope I didn't disturb you."

"I didn't hear a thing. The smell of coffee was nice though when I woke up."

"It was just this morning because I have jetlag", I promised. "I won't be awake so early in future - I hope not anyway."

She departed before long, I promised to text her when I knew what my plans were for the day.

At about 10:30 Frank responded to my text.

Would you like to come visit me today?

I texted back *Yes, where, and when?*

He gave me the address for his apartment/studio in Williamsburg and said to come as soon as possible. We settled on one pm, and I anxiously started sorting through my clothes deciding what to wear for this momentous meeting.

FORTY-TWO

The first thing I noticed was his height. He was tall. The second thing was his eyes. They were brown like mine. Nana, Uncle John, and his sons all had blue eyes. Even Tadhg had blue eyes. I had my father's eyes.

And the third thing was he seemed shy. He hesitated in the door arms extended as if to hug me, then stopped as if second-guessing himself. That endeared me as I realized the reticence, I had noticed in our phone calls, especially at the beginning, might have been shyness or fear of rejection.

I moved forward and hugged him. "Hello, at last!"

His arms closed around me, and he held me. Then he pulled back studying me face.

I laughed. "I have your eyes."

"Yes. Annie used to say that. She had blue eyes."

"I found a photo of her in the house in Ireland. She was a child. It was the only photo I ever saw of her. Nana didn't have any photos, so I never saw one of you or of my mother, not until I got to the house in Lockamore."

Frank stared at me in amazement. "You didn't even know what we looked like" he asked. "Well, I do have photos of her, and I will get copies for you."

"I want to see everything, hear everything" I said with conviction. "I am still shocked at Nana's behavior, but I have no more tolerance for secrets. I want to know everything."

"It is the only way forward", he agreed.

The story he told me was shocking. Several times I opened my mouth to protest.

My Nana! No! This couldn't be true!

But I said nothing, just let him talk.

*****

Frank began. "Tadhg told you how young he was when I was born. My parents were just sixteen. When I was twelve months my mother left home, and Tadhg took me to his parents. I was too young to remember that of course. But Frank and Eileen became my parents. Tadhg was away at college and then working. He didn't marry Joanne until I was twelve and then I chose to continue living with my grandparents, which I did until I was eighteen.

I'm telling you all of this so that you understand how close I was to Frank and Eileen. I called them Grandpa and Grandma, but it felt like they were my parents. Eileen always said how I looked so much like Frank when he was a young man. They told me stories about their childhood in Ireland. They would sit at night and talk to each other about people and places they had known in their youth, and I would listen.

I wanted to go to Art School and not go to college. This was not what the adults wanted. The compromise was that I would go to Art School for a year.   It would be a year off before going to college. I accepted, thinking they would change their minds in a year.

It was at a Gallery Opening in Saratoga that I met your mother. She was so beautiful, Una, like sunlight. We quickly fell in love. It was the summer after I had completed my first year at the art school. Annie was in college   We were both almost nineteen. Things developed quickly and a few months later we knew we wanted to be together.

The art school wasn't what I wanted but I wanted to paint. Annie was in college, but her heart wasn't in it. During the summer I had discovered an artist's colony where I could live and do my art. We decided that's what we would both do, move there if they would have us, and be together.

My family thought I was still at the art school. I must admit I was devious and let them think that, but Annie had been living at home. She had been in conflict with her mother. I didn't understand at that time the full extent of the problem. In any case, she desperately wanted to leave home and live with me.

Well, you know how religious your grandmother was. I thought at first, she was angry with me because I had influenced Annie to run away with me to "live in sin" as she put it. I didn't know at first that there was much more to it than that.

I had been seeing Annie for a few months before I met her mother. I was still at the art school in Albany. I went to pick her up at her house. We were going to visit the artist's colony, to have an interview to see if they would accept me. Annie was coming to give me her opinion, but I was hoping she might want to come too. She hadn't said yes yet. We had told nobody about this. Annie was adamant that she hadn't told her mother. I questioned her at length after that first meeting with her mother because her mother reacted so negatively to me.

"As soon as she saw you?" I asked.

"Well, yes. I thought at the time she took one look at me and didn't like what she saw. Later I realized that in that first moment Annie was also introducing me as Frank Donaghy".

"So, it was the name and how you looked. It must have been shocking to her" I said, as I thought of that story of Nana and the older Frank all those years ago.

"She stared at me and didn't say a word. Annie said later she was puzzled because her mother was usually very friendly. To help things along, Annie said that my people were from Cork too and I chimed in that my grandparents were born in Krumgedden, Co. Cork. That also produced a stony silence. We left shortly after that and in the car, I asked Annie what she had told her mother about our trip to the artist's colony. Annie said she had said nothing, just that we were going for a drive to Watkin's Glen. So honestly, we just forgot about it then. We were far too excited about our plans.

We liked the artist's group and the leader said we could both have a place there free of charge. We would have to share the cost of food and take our turn cooking and doing chores. We could move there in October if we wanted.   I was very excited, and Annie was open to trying it too.

Of course, when she announced to her mother that she was leaving home to stay with me, it produced a major reaction. I didn't hear all the details at first. I just knew that Annie's mother was furious. But we were caught up in our new life and I didn't think of it much.

A few years later, after you were born, Annie told me that her mother said that my grandfather Frank was a pervert, that he had molested children in her village, that he was forced to leave, that she wanted Annie to have nothing to do with me. I really don't know if Annie ever believed it, but she knew how attached I was to my grandfather. That was probably why she said nothing at first.

Annie did not stay in touch with her family, but I went to see Frank and Eileen regularly and I brought Annie with me. She liked them and was not happy about the deception. I let them think I was still at the art school in Albany for a couple of months. Then at Christmas when we saw them, I told them about the artists' colony, that I wanted to try it out. Tadhg was there and Joanne and he supported me saying I could go to college later if I wished and that I should explore this now if I felt so passionate about it.

"So, Annie, my mother, didn't communicate with her mother all that time?" I asked.

"That's right. She liked Frank and Eileen. It was only after you were born when we went to visit them once taking you with us that she told me about what her mother had said about Frank having molested children. I think she was troubled then, probably wondering if she should be concerned about you. Of course, I didn't believe it. I hated your grandmother for spreading a vicious lie, but it also planted some seeds of doubt. We never said anything but both Annie and I were careful to always stay close to you when we were visiting Frank and Annie."

"But it wasn't true!" I burst out. I couldn't stand it any longer. "It was a lie she made up."

Frank looked at me. "Yes, I believe that now, but we were very protective of you, so if we didn't really believe it, we still wanted to take no chances."

He doesn't know that Frank and Nana had a romantic involvement, and he has said nothing about Josie.

I decided to let him continue his story. I could fill him in later.

"Then there was the awful illness and death of your mother." His face was sad, voice strained. "It was so unbelievable, so shocking. We both decided to use herbs and natural remedies that were available locally and not see a doctor. We had no idea it was so serious. I did blame myself for that."

"What happened to her?" I asked.

"She had a miscarriage. It was late in the pregnancy. We

were both very sad about it, but we thought that even miscarriage was a natural process and didn't need medical attention. She hadn't seen a doctor throughout the pregnancy for that reason. And there was no doctor involved during her pregnancy with you. So naturally we thought this would be the same. We didn't understand that there could be complications from the miscarriage that would be fatal if untreated.

As well as the devastating loss of Annie there was the guilt that I was to blame, that she could have been saved if I insisted on a doctor before it was too late. Then there the police investigation of the artist's colony.

When your grandmother showed up to take you, I was in shock, and I let you go. I believed then I didn't deserve you, didn't deserve anything. I withdrew from everyone, somehow blaming Frank and Eileen for losing you. They were quite critical of me too that I didn't try to get medical help for Annie. I felt enough guilt already and I couldn't bear to be around them.

I tried to see you, but your grandmother refused, saying she would file an order of protection if I showed up. Your mother's death was still being investigated by the police and I was listed as a person of interest. I was ordered to not leave the area.

Eventually I was exonerated, and the focus shifted to the founder of the artist's colony. He was accused of putting pressure on very young people to experiment with drugs and to not seek medical attention when needed. But that took well over a year.

I was free to move then, and I wanted to go to New York. I wanted to start over away from everything familiar. I again approached your grandmother and said I was now ready to take you back to live with me. She was so cold, so angry. She threatened to file a civil case against me for causing Annie's death, and when she won, she would have custody of you because my family already had a record of having molested children in her family. She would make it all public and the family would be disgraced. That is when I learned about what Frank had done to her sister. I was so devastated then, I blamed him for losing you."

I stared at him in shock. "What did she say about Josie?"

"Was Josie her sister's name? Yes, I think I remember it was. She said Frank had stayed at their house working as a laborer. Josie was a child and Frank had molested her and was forced to leave. That was why he emigrated. I must say I felt then that I had nobody I could trust. My family that I had loved and trusted were despicable. I was despicable. I was responsible for the loss of this woman's only daughter. Could I be trusted to take care of a child? I thought you would be safer and happier with her. I felt I didn't deserve anything. I moved to New York, changed my name, and cut off contact with my family, except for Tadhg who eventually found me, and we started to connect gradually.

So that's the sad story."

Indeed, he looked sad. "I did think of you, particularly as time went on and I found solace in my art and gradually started feeling I wasn't so worthless after all, but your grandmother didn't relent. She still made the same threats even years later, so again I backed off."

I was white-faced with shock. My Nana who I had loved had done this! How many lives had she almost destroyed? How much pain had she caused?

Frank misinterpreted my facial expression. "I suppose you hate me now too. Maybe you are sorry you agreed to meet me.

"No!" I protested. "I am shocked at Nana's lies and destructiveness and vindictiveness. You see, none of it was true - about your grandfather molesting Josie I mean. It was something she made up to punish him. I know this because I met an old friend of hers when I was in Ireland, someone she confided in back then, someone she told at the time what she had convinced Josie to lie.

Nana was in love with Frank and when he rejected her to marry Eileen, she made up the story that he molested Josie and got Josie to believe it. There was never any molesting of children. But he did lose his job with her parents as a result, and he moved to England first and eventually to the States."

My father looked stunned. "None of it was true?" he said.

"No," I said sadly. "I could even have empathy for a seventeen-year-old girl who was heartbroken and lashed out vindictively in the moment, but when she saw the consequences, she didn't try to repair the damage. Who knows if she did irreparable damage to Josie, her own sister.?

"But to still be so vengeful so many years later," Frank said, shaking his head in amazement, "to punish her own daughter and granddaughter."

"It was almost forty years later" I said with surprise. Did she hate your grandfather so much after all that time that she would be so vindictive against you?"

"She was in pain at the death of Annie, and that was made worse by their estrangement for almost five years before Annie's death," Frank said. "At this point in time I can understand why she blamed me, why she hated me. As I said, I hated myself for a long time, and blamed myself. Maybe she really believed I was a dangerous person and that she needed to fight with whatever ammunition she had to protect you and to keep you safe."

He looked at me sadly. "She did love you, you know. I am sure of that."

"I don't know what to believe any more," I said. "I used to feel she loved me. I felt very close to her. I felt bereft when she died. But right now, I feel I was a pawn in a strange battle for revenge against your grandfather."

FORTY-THREE

You know, in an odd way there is a similarity to our stories" Frank said.

We were seated by the window in an Italian restaurant near his apartment where he had taken me after we were weary from talking. We were sipping wine and he was absent-mindedly nibbling on a breadstick while we waited for our dinner.

"You have another grandmother," Frank said, "my mother. I found her a few years ago, and we see each other sometimes. Because I felt so loved by Eileen and Frank and because I knew she had been so young when she had me, I didn't blame her for leaving, but I did for a long time feel resentful that she had made no attempt to see me in later years. Finally, I decided I should try to contact her. She was happy to meet me, had thought I would hate her and not want to know her."

I said nothing. I was still too hurt by what I had discovered about Nana. I didn't think I could cope with another grandmother right now.

He smiled. "I know this is a lot to absorb, but she lives in New York. Sometime when you are ready you might want to meet her."

"And I suppose your grandfather, Frank, is no longer alive", I said. I was changing the subject as I wasn't ready yet to commit myself to meeting my other grandmother, a woman who had also abandoned her baby.

"In fact, he is alive. I try to get back to visit him as often as I can. Eileen died a few years ago, so he is there on his own. After

Eileen died, I tried to spend more time with him. And again, I will not rush you, but I would love to bring you to see him when you feel ready."

I was fascinated that I could meet the man from that old photo, the man whose choices had such an impact on Nana's life and on my own too.

"Yes, I would like that, but not yet." I answered. "You know, all my life I wanted to know my father and his family, but when it started happening, I felt overwhelmed, still feel overwhelmed. I need a little time to get used to it. There is just so much to absorb."

"We share that," he said. "I still have difficulty being part of Tadhg and Joanne's family. Their children just don't feel like my family. I didn't grow up with them. Not that it is the same thing. I had most of my life to get used to them."

He continued, "But there is another similarity to our stories. I mean you are now disillusioned at seeing this other side to your Nana, just as I was when I thought Frank was a child molester."

"Except now you know for certain that was a lie and you can remember your happy childhood with him and know that was the real Frank, but I can't. The real Nana was a vindictive angry woman who kept me from my father". I said this bitterly. I was mourning the loss of a woman who never existed.

"She did this out of love for you though" Frank said with conviction. "Look, she believed I was not to be trusted, that I was irresponsible, a member of a cult, and that I had caused Annie's death. She thought she was saving you from someone who could be dangerous. She knew she was lying about my grandfather, but it was ammunition in her war. You know, 'all's fair in love and war,' that kind of thing. I am not saying I approve of her tactics, but I am certain she really loved you."

"I suppose so" I said sadly, "but all these lies, all that deception! All that time growing up knowing nothing about you or my mother."

"And she didn't have to leave the house to you" Frank continued. "Did you think of that? You said it was a complete surprise to you. You didn't know she had inherited the house. She could have arranged for it to be sold, even if that meant losing money and going against Ben's wishes. But she could have done that if she wanted to preserve her secrets.

But she didn't do that. She must have known you would go to Ireland and would learn the true story sooner or later. You would learn there were Donaghys in Krumgedden, and you would be curious about them. The lawyer who handled the inheritance for her is from Krumgedden. It would only be a matter of time before someone connected you with the Donaghy's there."

I looked at him in astonishment and said almost to myself, "The O'Sullivans live in Krumgedden - Fergal, his parents, and of course Matt must have been born there too. Yes, it was inevitable someone would figure it out eventually."

"Don't you think she wanted us to find each other in the end?" Frank said.

It was a ray of hope, a chance to heal my heart, and I grasped it.

ABOUT THE AUTHOR

Bailie Lawson has lived in Ireland and New York and loves to hear and to tell stories and to get lost in a book. She believes that stories shared are among the great pleasures of life, and a wonderful way to discover and share our common humanity.